Ellensburg

Enjoy!

J. M. Huff

Ellensburg

A. M. Huff

Ellensburg

A. M. Huff

Cover Design by J Caleb Design

This book was printed in the United States of America.

JaMarque Publishing, Redmond, Oregon

CONTENTS

DEDICATION

To my sister, Michael Anne Maslow.

ACKNOWLEDGMENTS

Special thanks to Dennis Blakesley, Barbara Larin-Blair, Melissa Ainsworth, Pamela Bainbridge-Cowan, Ruth Bradley, Chris Forcier, Anthony Huff, Pushpa Huff, Phyllis Jensen, Betsy Jones, Kathleen Mooney, Bill Ray and Lea Sevey for their encouragement and support.

CHAPTER ONE

Harrison glanced in his rearview mirror for the umpteenth time since leaving work. Ever since waking up that morning he'd had a strange feeling like someone was watching him. It was unnerving. Nevertheless, to be safe, he took another route home, even stopping at a small grocery store to buy things he didn't really need. After circling his block a couple times, Harrison finally pulled into his driveway and shut off the engine.

Harrison picked the grocery bags up from the passenger seat of his VW Bug. Even though they were awkward and heavy, he managed to hold all three plastic bags with his left hand, leaving his right hand free to unlock the back door of his old, two-story, Portland Craftsman home. As usual, after turning off the ignition, he put his keys into the left pocket of his slacks. Instantly he heard the familiar voice in his head, *one trip Harry.*

"Damn! Why do I always do that?"

Instead of setting the sacks down on the concrete steps or shifting them to his right hand, Harrison awkwardly twisted, reached across himself and dug at the keys with his right hand. Inside the house he could hear the telephone begin to ring.

"Coming!" he yelled though the locked door and dug more frantically. A sharp pain in his right shoulder reminded him that his arms had their limits and he was close to dislocating one of them. When the telephone rang again, he ignored the pain and worked the keys up to the top of his pocket. They slipped through his fingers and clanked as they hit the steps. Bouncing, they ended up in the flowerbed below.

"Really?" he groaned and scooped them up along with a sliver from the bark dust.

Opening the door into the kitchen he hurriedly dropped the grocery bags on the island and grabbed for the telephone.

"Hello?"

The buzz of the dial tone answered him. He was too late. He looked at the small caller display, *Unknown.*

"Damn it!" he cursed and returned the handset to its charger. The fog suddenly lifted and he remembered. It wasn't a feeling that someone was following him, watching him. It was the feeling that something wasn't right, like the morning when the hospital called to tell them his mother had died. The realization didn't make the feeling go away, instead it intensified.

Col. Mustard strolled into the kitchen and looked at Harrison with large orange eyes.

"Sorry about that. I guess whomever it was will just have to call back. You want some dinner?"

Col. Mustard didn't answer. He just stared at Harrison and sat down on the floor in front of the foyer doorway.

"Oh brother, he's only been gone for three days and already I've been reduced to talking to a *cat*." Harrison chided himself.

Col. Mustard licked his paw and began grooming himself.

Harrison closed the back door and turned his attention to the three grocery bags. It didn't take long to unpack the groceries. Col. Mustard appeared to be disinterested until Harrison pressed on the can opener and the seal on the can of cat food popped. Suddenly Col. Mustard found his voice and mewed incessantly.

"All right, all right, you're not starving to death. Even though you're acting like it. Do you give Thomas as bad a time as this?" Harrison set the small cat dish on the floor by the water bowl. Col. Mustard all but pushed him out of the way in his rush to get to the food.

Harrison shook his head and watched his pet eat for a moment before he poured himself a glass of White Zinfandel. He took a large sip and opened the door of the fridge. Nothing looked good and if it did, it felt like too much work to go through for only one. He closed the door and decided to order a pizza delivered.

Hanging up the telephone Harrison looked at the clock on the wall above the fridge. He had twenty minutes before dinner would arrive. Rushing into his bedroom, he shed clothes. Grabbing his robe, he headed for the shower in the hall bathroom. The hot water felt good on his neck and shoulders. He basked in its warmth for a moment before grabbing the soap. After rinsing himself, he reluctantly shut the water off. If only he had a few more minutes it would be nice to linger and let the water relax him a bit more.

Back in his bedroom, he grabbed his favorite pair of blue jeans, the pair that was torn in one knee and worn along the bottom hem in both legs. *But they were comfortable*, he reminded himself. He pulled an old, faded OSU sweatshirt, a gift from his sister Danika, over his head. Looking in the mirror above his dresser, he ran a comb through his hair. He frowned at his reflection. He didn't feel old enough to have grey hair, but there it was. He turned away from his reflection and started to slip on his tennis shoes. He stopped and changed his mind, preferring to go barefoot instead.

Walking into the living room he looked through the bookcase of DVD's. They were a bone of contention between Thomas and him. Thomas never understood how anyone could possibly enjoy watching a movie they had already seen countless times.

"You already know how it's gonna end," Thomas always said and shook his head. "It's just a waste of time."

Harrison had given up trying to explain it to him ages ago.

He finally settled on his favorite movie of all time. He had seen it so many times over the years he had lost count; and even though he had memorized the dialog, he still enjoyed watching it play out, especially on a dreary fall evening like that night. He popped the DVD into the player and went to retrieve his glass of wine and the bottle from the kitchen while the intro played.

Just when he was about to enter the living room, the front doorbell rang. Quickly he set the glass and bottle down on the sideboard in the foyer and answered the door.

"Hi there," greeted the young man standing on the front porch with a large oven bag in one hand. Harrison smiled and nodded. "You ordered a pizza?"

"That I did," Harrison answered. He reached in the back pocket of his jeans for his wallet. "Come in for a sec," he invited and stepped back to allow the young man to enter. "I left my wallet in the other room. I'll be right back." Harrison rushed back to his bedroom where he had left his wallet on the dresser.

When he returned to the foyer, the young man was standing in the archway to the living room watching the TV.

"What movie is that?" he asked.

"The Poseidon Adventure," Harrison answered proudly.

"Oh, is that the one with Kurt Russell?"

"No," Harrison smiled and felt ancient. "It's the original version with Gene Hackman and Shelley Winters."

A puzzled look came over the delivery boy's face. "I don't think I've seen that one."

"Well, you'll have to check it out, sometime." Harrison opened his wallet.

The young man smiled and then with the agility of someone who had done it a million times before, he spun the oven bag around, opened it, releasing the mouth-watering aroma of melted cheese, tomato sauce and sausage. He removed the flat box, tucking the empty bag between his legs. He opened the box and held it up for Harrison to inspect.

"It smells wonderful and looks delicious," Harrison told him.

The young man closed the box. "That'll be twenty-one fifty."

Feeling generous, Harrison handed him a twenty and a ten. "Keep the change."

The delivery boy looked at the money and then back at Harrison with a big smile. "Thanks."

Balancing the pizza box in one hand, Harrison opened the front door with his other.

The young man glanced back at the TV one last time.

"Maybe you can show me the movie sometime?" he said and smiled coyly, biting his lower lip.

"Maybe," Harrison answered and immediately felt nervous. *Is this boy flirting with me? I'm old enough to be his father and why would he think I would be interested?*

The young man stepped back out onto the front porch and turned around. "You can reach me at the number on the back of the card." He handed Harrison a business card from Abby's Pizza with a phone number written on the back.

This kid was definitely flirting, Harrison thought.

"Thank you," he answered to be polite.

"Good night, sir, and enjoy your pizza."

Harrison closed the door and leaned against it. He looked at the card again and then at Col. Mustard who had rushed into the foyer at the first whiff of sausage. "Sir?" he said looking at Col. Mustard for support. "Nothing like making me feel like an old man."

Harrison traded the card for his bottle of wine which he tucked under his arm. Then he grabbed his glass carefully, keeping enough pressure on the bottle so it wouldn't slip. Col Mustard, who normally ignored him, kept mewing and rubbing against Harrison's legs.

"I know what you want," Harrison told him with a laugh. "You're not fooling anyone."

Harrison sat down on the sofa across from the large leaded-glass window in the living room. He set the pizza box on the glass-top coffee table and then grabbed the wine bottle. He set it safely beside the pizza. With a big gulp of wine, he grabbed the remote and restarted the movie. Col. Mustard jumped up on the sofa beside Harrison and stretched his neck to get his nose closer to the pizza.

"Okay, just this once. Don't tell Thomas," Harrison laughed. He picked a few pieces of sausage from a slice of pizza and put them on a coaster for Col. Mustard and then settled back on the sofa to watch the movie and eat and drink himself into a stupor.

The sound of the telephone ringing startled Harrison out of his sleep. His heart pounding in his chest, he looked around the living room confused about where he was. The television was still on, showing an illuminated blank screen with the Samsung logo bouncing around. The pizza box sat closed on the coffee table with a half-empty bottle of wine and wine glass sitting beside it.

The phone rang again. Harrison jumped up only to fall flat on the floor, his legs tangled in the Pendleton wool throw he didn't remember covering himself with. After he freed his legs, he rushed into the dining room to retrieve the phone.

"Hello?"

"Thomas?"

"No, this is Harrison."

"Oh, is Thomas there?" The woman's tone turned icy.

"I'm sorry, he's not here right now. May I know who's calling?"

"His mother."

Now her tone made sense to Harrison. Mrs. Unger never approved of his friendship with her son. *"What sort of man isn't married by the time he's thirty?"* she asked Thomas when she thought Harrison couldn't hear. *"You shouldn't get too close to that kind. People will start thinking you're that way too."* Thomas repeatedly told his mother she was wrong and that there was nothing going on between Harrison and him. *"No one lets another person live with them rent free and not expect something in return,"* she insisted. Thomas explained that the house belonged to Harrison's parents and that he inherited it. It was paid for, so Harrison didn't feel he needed to charge rent. Still Mrs. Unger was not convinced.

"Hi, Mrs. Unger," Harrison said trying to sound cheerful. "Thomas left Tuesday. He's not there?"

"Would I be calling if he were?"

"No, I suppose not. He left at seven and told me he was taking the coast route. He was staying overnight in Ellensburg. He should have been to your place—"

"But obviously he's not."

"He has his cell phone—"

"I tried that already. He didn't answer. Obviously you're no help. If you hear from him, tell him to call me. I'm worried."

"I will."

The phone went dead. Harrison imagined had it been one of those older sets, like the one his parents had when he was growing up, he would have heard the receiver slam down. He turned the receiver off and put it back on the charger.

Walking back into the living room, the realization hit him. The uneasiness he had been feeling was about Thomas. Harrison turned off the television and scooped up the pizza box, wine bottle and glass. Col. Mustard, curled up on the fringes of the blanket, opened his eyes and gave his "master" a disgusted look before going back to sleep.

Col. Mustard was Harrison's cat, at least on paper at the vet's office. Usually he slept curled up on Thomas' bed. In Thomas' absence, he begrudgingly slept on the end of the sofa. The only time he interacted with Harrison was when he wanted his food, or his litter box cleaned. Then his yowling was relentless.

What Harrison couldn't understand was Thomas would cradle Col. Mustard like a baby, kiss his little forehead and nuzzle him, and even rub his belly. If Harrison tried to do the same, he earned himself multiple scratches for his thanks.

Instead, Col. Mustard would follow Thomas around the house, sit on his lap for hours and glare at Harrison.

After tossing the empty pizza box into the recycle bin, Harrison decided against disturbing Col. Mustard and left the blanket bunched up on the sofa. Instead he went into the den and turned on his computer monitor. He hadn't checked his emails the night before and suddenly remembered Thomas had taken his laptop, perhaps he emailed.

The telephone rang again. Harrison grabbed the extension and answered it without looking at the caller id.

"Hello?"

"Hi there."

He recognized her voice immediately and rocked back in his office chair.

"Hi, sis, what's up?"

"Oh, nothing much. I just wanted to see how your weekend is going."

"I take it *he's* not home."

"Harry, why do you have to be like that?"

"Because I don't like him."

"You did when I married him."

"That was before he started cheating on you and hitting you."

"That was a long time ago and to be fair, I was spending long hours at work—"

"That's no excuse and you know it. How many cases of spousal abuse have you handled?"

"I didn't call to argue with you." Her tone was sharp and blunt.

"I know, I'm sorry, Dani. I guess I'm just a bit stressed at the moment."

"Why? What's going on?"

"Thomas left for San Diego four days ago. His mother called saying he hasn't arrived."

"Well, maybe he's taking his time?"

"I guess, but I haven't heard from him. He usually calls me every night to tell me where he's staying. Just so if anything happens I know where to send the police."

"Have you tried calling him?"

"Yes. It goes to his voice mail and his mother has filled it up."

"What way was he going?"

"He was taking the coast route. He said he likes the scenery better than going down I-5."

"Well, I wouldn't worry too much. He probably stopped to visit friends or take in the scenery."

"I don't know. I guess you're probably right. How are the boys?"

"Growing like weeds. Bobby is quite the little man. He is such a help with Timmy."

"That's good."

"Oh I'll talk to you later."

"Okay. I love—"

Again the telephone went dead in Harrison's hand. He hung it up and glanced at the doorway. Col. Mustard was awake and staring at him.

"Suppose you want your breakfast?"

Col. Mustard mewed and turned toward the kitchen.

Harrison could barely get the bowl to the placemat on the floor before Col. Mustard attacked it. Sneakily, Harrison let his hand slide down Col. Mustard's back, feeling his soft fur, while Col. Mustard was distracted by the food. Still, Harrison could feel his pet cringe and try to move away. He even yowled in protest but kept his face buried in his bowl.

"You are such a nut," Harrison laughed. He turned away and made a pot of coffee.

Today was Saturday. Harrison had the whole weekend to himself to relax but he couldn't. Not only was he already worried about Thomas, but now he found himself worrying about Danika as well.

He never would have believed that Robert would turn out the way he had. When he met his sister's fiancé, a week before the wedding, Robert had just been promoted to sergeant on the Virginia Beach Police force. He was the perfect gentleman. He doted on Danika. He opened doors for her. He pulled out her chair at the restaurant. There weren't any red flags.

Harrison kicked himself now. He should have been a better brother. Danika had confided in him, while standing in the bridal room at the church in her wedding gown, that she was having second thoughts about marrying Robert. Like a typical bachelor and fool, he told her it was just nerves. *Cold feet. Everyone gets them,* his words echoed in his ears. *How the hell would I know?*

Even when she came out and said, "I don't want to marry him," Harrison didn't hear it. Instead he talked her down the aisle and into the arms of the lowest form of a human being.

That was eight years, two babies, three broken ribs and numerous black eyes ago. Eight years of Harrison feeling like he failed her and their parents. After their parents died, their mother from a heart attack, their father from drinking himself to death due to his grief, Harrison had taken on the task of looking out for her. He always said that once she was married he would get on with his life. Was he in too much of a hurry that he pushed her into an unhappy marriage just so he could have a life of his own?

Harrison poured himself a cup of coffee and picked up the telephone. Without having to think about it, he dialed Thomas' cell number. It rang and immediately was answered.

"The mailbox you've reached is full," the woman's voice announced.

"Damn it!" He cursed Thomas' mother.

He glanced at Col. Mustard while he put the phone back on its charger. He was finished eating and was busy washing his face with his paw.

"All done?" Harrison said, as if talking to a baby. Col. Mustard ignored him and continued grooming himself.

Harrison picked up the cat dish and rinsed it out in the sink.

Walking back into the living room he stood staring at the television, the coffee table, and sofa. Everything was neatly in its place except the blanket that belonged on the back of the sofa. He thought about folding it but the task felt too overwhelming.

Why doesn't he call?

He thought about going for a walk around the neighborhood for some fresh air and to get away from the thoughts in his head but decided not to. *It's about to rain anyway*, he excused himself.

Sitting in front of his computer, the cursor blinking against a white page, he couldn't even collect his thoughts enough to work on his novel.

Damn it! Where are you, Thomas?

He bolted forward in his chair as a thought suddenly came to him. He pulled up the internet browser and clicked on the bookmark for the bank he and Thomas used. He typed in Thomas' user name and password and instantly the account information popped up.

"If you won't call me, then I will track you this way," Harrison said aloud to himself. "Let's see if you stuck to your habit."

If Thomas had, then he would use his credit card for all his purchases along the way. *I want to save my cash for San Diego, plus I earn fuel points.*

Harrison's stomach tightened. The last purchase had been four days ago, for gas purchased in Port Orford.

"Damn it, Thomas," he cursed and hit the print icon.

CHAPTER TWO

When Harrison walked into his office in the U.S. Bank Tower in downtown Portland—well, more a cubicle in the corner of a larger office that took up most of the east half of the twenty-eighth floor—he was greeted by his co-worker.

"Morning," Justus smiled and plopped down on the corner of Harrison's desk.

"Get off my desk," Harrison groused.

"Oh, someone's had a bad weekend," Justus teased and hopped down.

Harrison looked at the file clerk and suddenly couldn't believe how incredibly young he seemed. It wasn't just because Justus was a reed-thin, five feet six and a whole head shorter than Harrison. Justus didn't look old enough to shave. His smooth skin, short wavy hair, thick eyebrows and nearly coal black eyes instantly brought flashes of the photos of JFK Jr. to Harrison's mind. Justus wasn't even out of diapers when that young man died. Harrison felt ancient.

"What?" Justus asked.

Suddenly, Harrison realized that he'd been staring at his file clerk. He shook his head and sat down. He kept his back to the wall and the windows to his left. Harrison hated heights. It took him months if not years to get used to the elevators rocketing him up to the twenty-eighth floor and even twice as long to be able to get within six feet of the windows. Still, he could not bring himself to turn his back on them.

"So, are you going to tell me about your weekend?" Justus persisted.

"No," Harrison answered and realized he sounded tired, which he was. Between worrying about Thomas and feeling guilty about how he over-reacted when Danika called, he hadn't gotten much rest. He was grateful for the distraction of work.

"Oh, that bad, eh?" Justus sympathized. Once again, he sat down on the edge of Harrison's wooden desk and folded his arms around the files he was holding. "So, wanna hear about my weekend?"

"Sure," Harrison answered in a less-than-enthused tone, knowing that even if he had said, no, Justus would tell him anyway.

"Friday night I went to the club and met this hot guy. We danced and talked. He wouldn't let me pay for my drinks. Isn't that so cool?"

"I suppose," Harrison answered while he looked through a file on his desk.

"He wanted to come back to my place—"

Harrison looked up. "Don't you still live with your parents?"

"Yeah, I know, but I couldn't tell him that. So, I told him I'd rather see where he lives."

"You didn't," Harrison pretended to be shocked.

15

"I did."

"Slut." Harrison whispered so no one other than Justus would hear.

Justus laughed and leaned closer. "It was the best sex I ever had. You wouldn't believe the size of his co—"

"Okay, that's enough," Harrison interrupted. He could feel his cheeks turning red. "We're at work and I don't need all the gory details."

"Condo." Justus finished and sat back giving a slight giggle. "What did you think I was going to say?"

"Fine," Harrison said and shook his head. He knew exactly what Justus was going to say. The fact that he changed his mind mid-word wasn't fooling him. "I have work to do and so do you. Best not let the boss catch you doing nothing."

"Okay. Lunch?" Justus asked and stood up.

"Don't we always?"

"Just checking," Justus almost sang while he bounced his way out of Harrison cubicle.

All morning Harrison tried to focus on his work but found that even that was a challenge and a bit more difficult than he expected. No matter how hard he tried, his mind kept going back to Thomas. *Where could he be?*

"Ready for lunch?"

"Sure," Harrison answered and scribbled something down on a page then closed the file. "I'll hand this off to Debra on our way out. She's been bugging me all morning for it."

"What is it?" Justus asked.

"It's the annual service billing for one of my major accounts. I've been working on it for the past two hours—" He shook his head. "I can't understand how it could get so messed up. It took me an hour to straighten it out."

"Good, now forget about it for the next hour. Let's just

relax and have our lunch."

Harrison dropped the file in the in-basket on Debra's desk and headed down to the main floor of the bank tower building.

The plaza level reminded Harrison of any one of the shopping malls around Portland. Stores and shops lined the outside walls with main entrances facing the courtyard in the center. Large green palm trees and bushes occupied the many giant concrete planters that brought the outside in. Patio tables and chairs sat clustered in the center of the courtyard with plenty of walking space on either side.

"I'll grab our table," Justus said when they both saw the line outside their favorite eatery. "Get me the usual."

"Chicken rice bowl, no veggie, light sauce, got it." Harrison confirmed and went to stand in line.

Being surrounded by so many noisy people did little to drown out the uneasy thoughts that flooded his mind. Harrison felt his stomach knot. He took out his cell phone and dialed the voice message retrieval number for his home phone. He keyed in his password.

"You have no new messages and no saved messages," the semi-cheerful female voice informed him.

He disconnected and then dialed Thomas' number. The same voice informed him that Thomas' mailbox was full.

"Where are you?" Harrison said out loud and disconnected the call.

The man standing in line in front of him turned around. "What?"

"Oh, I'm sorry. Just talking to myself," Harrison admitted.

"Do that often?" the man asked with a smile.

"Only when I'm really stressed," Harrison answered

feeling stupid.

He stepped up to the counter and placed his order then realized Justus had done it again, left him to pay for lunch. Harrison shook his head and handed the cashier his bankcard.

"Yoo-hoo, over here," Justus called from across the courtyard in a high pitched tone more befitting a woman. As if that weren't bad enough, he also added a double-handed wave.

Harrison felt his face turn red when he noticed the staring crowd around him. He ducked and hurried over to the table.

"Why do you insist on embarrassing me?" he said while he set the tray down.

Justus giggled. "Because I think it's cute seeing a man of your age blush."

"I'm not that old," Harrison said and sat down. The metal feet on the chair made a sharp scraping sound against the polished concrete floor. "Couldn't you find another chair?" he lamented.

"All the others were taken." Justus took the plastic lid off his bowl and released the steam and aroma of his teriyaki chicken over white rice. "They gave me a huge piece of chicken this time."

"Yeah, I guess they felt sorry for me having to wait so long."

"So, are you gonna tell me what's going on?" Justus asked and then stuck a forkful of rice coated chicken into his mouth.

"I really don't want to talk about it."

"Don't tell me something happened to Col. Mustard?"

"No. He's fine."

"Get a parking ticket?"

"No."

18

"Find out you caught V.D.?"

Harrison glared at Justus.

"Come on, what's eating you? I can tell something is."

"You wouldn't understand," Harrison said while he picked at the rice and chicken in his bowl with his plastic fork.

"I really hate that." Justus' tone became cold and bordered on angry. "My mom says that a lot. I'm not a child. I'm twenty-freaking-one years old. I'm your friend for god's sake."

Harrison looked at his co-worker. For the past two years they'd had lunch together nearly every day, chatting about life, well, mostly Justus' life. Were they really friends now?

"Okay, I'm sorry," Harrison surrendered to the idea. "Last Tuesday my friend Thomas went to see his mother in San Diego. She called me Saturday morning and said he hadn't arrived yet."

"Oh, the dreaded mother-in-law," Justus teased.

"She's not my mother-in-law, knock it off!" Harrison growled. "I've told you, Thomas is my boarder. We're friends, nothing more."

"Okaaay," Justus answered, drawing out the word and making it sound as though he still was not convinced.

"Just stop it or I won't say another word," Harrison warned and put the lid over his untouched lunch bowl.

"Did you try calling him?"

"Yes, but I only reached his voice mail and the box is full. Apparently his mother has filled it up with her incessant calling. My guess is once it no longer answered, she called me."

"I take it he hasn't called you."

"No." Harrison shook his head and kept staring at the warm rice bowl he cradled in his hands.

"You don't think something's happened do you?"

"I don't know. Maybe. He takes the coast route. I've taken that route before. Sometimes there are slides that wipe out a chunk of the road. In other places the road gets really narrow and there are steep cliffs and tall bridges."

"Oh my, what if his car went over the edge!"

Harrison looked at Justus with disapproving eyes. "Not helping."

"Oh, sorry. So, what are you going to do?"

"I don't know. What can I do?"

"Go to the police. File a missing person report."

"That was a rhetorical question," Harrison said but then thought about it. "Do you think they can do anything?"

"Hell yeah! They can put out one of those amber alert thingies."

"They only do that for missing children and he's not a child."

"Well, maybe they can do a *grey* alert or whatever they do when an old person goes missing."

"He's not elderly. He's thirty-one."

"Well, that's old."

"Watch it, buckwheat. You'll be thirty-one before you know it."

"Never! I'm going to stay twenty-one forever. At least that's what I'm going to tell everyone." Justus laughed.

"Well, we best head back."

When the two were alone in the elevator, Justus turned toward Harrison.

"Seriously, all kidding aside, you should go to the police."

"I'll think about it."

The afternoon seemed to drag on. Harrison tried to

focus his thoughts on his work but now all he could think about was going to the police. What would he say? What would they do? Could they really help him?

He shoved his paperwork aside and pulled his keyboard closer. He accessed his personal email account, something he knew the boss frowned upon but which was not totally out of line. He scanned the messages for one from Thomas. Nothing. Just before logging out he noticed an email from Danika. He opened it.

"Hey Harrison,

Sorry for rushing off the other day. Robert came home, you know…

Anyway, I have to take the boys to school. I'll call you later.

Love you,

Dani"

Harrison rocked back in his chair and stared at his computer screen. He didn't know what to think about Danika's email. It really didn't say much but it confirmed what he had suspected about the abrupt end to their telephone conversation. He sat forward and logged out of his email account. Grabbing his coffee mug he went to the break room.

The moment he walked into the windowless room in the center of the twenty-eighth floor he spotted Justus across the room with his counterpart from upstairs. She appeared to be doing all of the talking while Justus stood listening.

Harrison ignored them and poured himself a cup of coffee. At this hour of the day it was decaf. A group of women in the office had insisted on it and the boss, always looking to get lucky, caved. Harrison added three vanilla creamers and headed back to his desk.

Just before quitting time, Justus slipped into Harrison's

cubicle. Harrison glanced at him then turned his attention back to the file that was spread out before him.

Justus walked around the desk and sat himself down on his customary corner, then leaned closer to Harrison and whispered.

"I was just talking to Victoria in the breakroom."

"I know, I saw you two."

Justus sat up for a second, looking confused, then shook his head and leaned back.

"You can't trust Debra," he continued.

"Why?" Harrison asked while he straightened the small stack of papers and put them back into their file.

"Victoria said she saw Debra in Eric's office and neither of them were happy."

"So, what's that got to do with me?" Harrison shut off his computer and bumped Justus' knee to get him to move out of the way. Justus did and Harrison opened his desk drawer and stuck the file inside.

"Victoria said she heard Debra say your name."

"Whatever. I don't care. Debra is just a brown-noser. I wouldn't be surprised if she were doing him just to get a promotion."

"Eew!" Justus recoiled and looked as if he were going to lose his lunch.

"Justus, thank you for telling me. I will keep it in mind but right now I have more pressing matters to think about."

"Say, speaking of that, are you going to go to the police?"

"I don't know. Maybe. But before I do, I need to check with his mother and his friends in San Francisco first. Maybe he stopped there on his way to San Diego." Harrison slipped into his jacket and made sure his keys were still in his pocket before starting for the elevators.

"So, when are you going to call them?"

"You're sure a pushy little snot!" Harrison shook his head and pressed the down button.

"Well, what if he's broken down on the side of the road somewhere and there's no cell service? Or worse, what if he picked up a hitchhiker with an axe?"

"You watch too many movies, Justus."

The doors opened and the two joined the crowd inside. Justus hadn't told Harrison anything he hadn't already thought of first, except the hitchhiker axe thing. Thomas was generous but not when it came to his precious Cadillac. After *the incident*, as it became known, no one was allowed to ride in it, especially some sweaty, dusty stranger. No, Thomas wouldn't pick up a hitchhiker.

The two men parted ways once they left the building. Justus headed for the bus mall while Harrison headed for the parking garage three blocks away.

The early evening sun was obscured by the West Hills and the tall buildings but there was still enough light to keep the streetlights from switching on. Harrison stopped at the intersection of Fourth and Oak while he waited for the "Don't Walk" sign to change. He looked at the grey stone building and read the sign on the corner, Portland City Police. Funny, he had never really noticed it before, never had a reason to. He walked up to the front doors and went inside.

The lobby was actually quieter than he had imagined. The TV shows must have it wrong, or at least they didn't know about Portland's police. *Now who watches too much television?*

He walked across the lobby to a window with a metal speaker in the center of the glass, the kind he remembered seeing in the old movie theater ticket office when he was a boy. A police woman stepped into view.

"May I help you?" she asked leaning toward the metal speaker.

"I don't know. My roommate went to visit his mother and hasn't been heard from since."

"I see," she answered and looked rather bored. "How long ago was this?"

"Last Tuesday."

"How old is this person?"

"He's thirty-one."

"Does he have a medical condition or anything that would be a cause for concern?"

"No."

"Do you have any reason to suspect there has been a crime committed or that any harm has come to him?"

"No. Not really. I'm just worried because I haven't been able to reach him, and his mother phoned last Saturday and said he hasn't arrived."

"Saturday? Where does his mother live?"

"San Diego."

"Oh, well, that changes things. Unless there is a suspicion that a crime has been committed, or that your friend is in any danger of harming himself or anyone else, there's not much we can do. He's a healthy man. Perhaps he decided to go sightseeing or changed his mind and went somewhere else."

"But I checked his bank account and he hasn't used his credit card since he got gas in Port Orford several days ago." Harrison pulled the folded up paper from the inside pocket of his suitcoat to show the policewoman.

She gave it a polite glance when he held it against the glass. "Well, maybe he's paying cash for things."

"No. He told me he was going to put it all on his Visa to get the points."

"Well, Port Orford is way out of our jurisdiction. Perhaps you should check with the police there."

"But I thought—"

"Most people do." She cut Harrison off.

He just looked at her. He couldn't believe she wasn't willing to at least take a missing person report. The policewoman stared back at him with no feeling in her eyes.

"Is there anything else?" she asked sounding a bit annoyed that he was still standing at her window.

"No, I guess not." Harrison answered. Folding up the paper, he jammed it into the front pocket of his coat. His opinion of Portland's Finest dropped another notch. Turning around he left without another word.

Once home, with Col. Mustard given his dinner, Harrison settled on the sofa with a glass of wine and tried to think of someone who would actually listen and help. The first name that came to him was Thomas' and his mutual friend Mike. Picking up the phone and dialed from memory. The sound of a ringing phone replaced the buzz of the dial tone.

"Hello."

"Hi, Mike, this is Harrison."

"Hey, Harrison, long time no chat! How've you been?"

"Oh, pretty good. Say, the reason I'm calling is I was wondering if you've seen or heard from Thomas?"

"No I haven't. I've been in Vegas for the last week. Why?"

"He left last Tuesday for his mother's and I haven't been able to reach him and he hasn't called. I thought he might have stopped at your place but if you were out of town . . ."

"Oh," Mike sounded concerned for a moment and then he laughed as though to hide it. "His mother's probably got him tied up doing god-knows-what for her. You know how she can be."

"True," Harrison agreed. Mrs. Unger did monopolize her son. She always claimed she wanted to see him married but in reality if it ever actually happened she would be miserable. "But I don't think so. She called here last Saturday saying Thomas hasn't arrived."

"Oh?" This time Mike didn't try to hide the concern in his voice. "Well, that does change things a bit. But, I guess we shouldn't be too worried. I'll check with Jenny and Bill. Maybe he stopped by their place."

"I'd appreciate it."

"So when are you gonna come down? We had such a great time the last time you did."

"Yeah, how many movies did we see, twenty?"

"Twenty-nine," Mike corrected, drawing out the words.

"Good grief. That's quite a feat in five days. I thought Thomas was going to kill us by the time our vacation was over."

Mike laughed. "Hey, I've gotta go. Company's here and you know…"

"Yeah. Be safe." I answered. "Talk to you later."

"I'll let you know what I find out and, you let me know if you find him first."

"I will."

Harrison hung up. Walking into the kitchen, he refilled his wine glass and took a large gulp. His next call was the one he dreaded most, but he had to do it. He dialed the number and pressed "Talk". The phone rang once.

"Unger residence," the woman's voice greeted him.

"Mrs. Unger? This is Harrison, Thomas' friend."

"I know who you are," came her icy response.

Harrison ignored it and began to pace around the small island in the middle of the kitchen.

"I was wondering if you've heard from Thomas yet?"

"No, I haven't. I take it, since you are calling, that you haven't either. So, what are you doing about it?"

Harrison's stomach tightened into what was beginning to feel like its customary knot, while his head had begun to feel the effects of the wine.

"I tried going to the police but they referred me to the local police in Port Orford."

"Port Orford? Why there?"

"Because it was the last place he bought gas with his Visa card."

"How do you know that?" she demanded.

"Because I have access to his account on line," Harrison blurted before he had a chance to think of a better answer.

"You what?" Mrs. Unger nearly screamed.

"For emergency purposes we both have access to each other's account." Harrison explained and cringed while he waited for her to scream again.

"Have you tried going to the state police up there?" she asked in a calmer but still frosty tone.

"Not yet."

"Good God, what are you waiting for? You're supposed to be his friend. For heaven's sake act like it, call the state police, now!"

Again the line went dead, just as it always did when Harrison had the misfortune of talking to her. He set his phone down and finished off his glass of wine in one gulp.

For what seemed like hours he paced the kitchen floor

before he picked up the telephone again. He dialed the number for directory assistance.

"What city please?"

"Portland, I guess. I need the non-emergency number for the state police."

"One moment. Would you like the number or for me to connect you?"

"Connect me, please."

The phone on the other end began to ring.

"Oregon State Police, how may I direct your call?"

"I need to report a missing person."

"One moment."

Over the next twenty minutes Harrison felt as if he were talking to the male version of the policewoman he'd talked to in downtown Portland earlier. While the officer gave the pretense of being sympathetic, he didn't sound the least bit concerned. Harrison hung up feeling just as lost and helpless as before.

CHAPTER THREE

The next morning, Harrison walked into his office exhausted. The conversation with the police the night before still weighed heavily on his mind causing him to feel more anxious every minute. He stopped at the edge of the partition that separated his workspace from the rest of the office. For a moment he idly watched Justus straightening a stack of files.

"Where did those come from?" Harrison asked and started to take off his sport coat.

"Ah, you might want to leave that on," Justus said, ignoring Harrison's question.

"What's going on? What are you doing with those files?"

"Remember I warned you to be careful around Debra?"

"Yeah, so?"

"Well, Eric wants to see you in his office."

Harrison gave Justus a puzzled look. "What about?"

"I'm not sure, but Debra was with him when he told me to tell you. And, she threw these on your desk."

Harrison took a closer look at the folders. They were out

of the file cabinet behind his desk.

"How did she get these?" he asked.

"Don't know. I left with you last night, remember?"

"Yeah," Harrison nodded. "Did Eric say when he wanted to see me?"

"He just told me to tell you the minute you came in. I assume that means he wants you now?"

Harrison drew a deep breath. "Okay. Wish me luck."

"You know you have it."

Instead of taking the elevator up the one floor, Harrison opted for the stairs. At least if he fell, it would only be to the floor versus twenty-nine stories down. The higher Harrison climbed, the more his legs shook. He tried not to think about it and pressed on.

The stairwell door opened to a wide hallway with the elevators to the left and doors, some solid wood and others glass, dotting the walls on either side, up and down. Harrison knew the way to his boss' office though he hadn't had reason to visit it in ages.

He opened the milk-glass door and walked into the reception room. Mrs. Cox, Eric's secretary, sat behind her desk with earbuds on while she typed into her computer. When she saw Harrison enter, she pulled one of the buds out and gave him a welcoming smile.

"Good Morning," she greeted in a cheerful tone.

Harrison wondered why, with Eric's womanizing ways, he had hired a woman old enough to be his mother for his secretary. Not that Mrs. Cox wasn't attractive which. For a woman of her late fifties, she certainly was, but she just didn't seem to fit. *Perhaps she came with the position,* Harrison thought.

"I understand that Mr. Meyers wants to see me?"

"Yes. Just a moment." Her smile never wavered. She lifted the receiver on her rather large desktop phone and pressed a button. "Mr. Andrews is here," she announced. "I will," she answered and then put the receiver back on its cradle. "Go right in."

Unlike the cubicles downstairs, Eric Meyers had an actual office with four solid walls and a door. Harrison didn't know why but he felt uneasy every time he visited Eric in there. Perhaps because, when the door was shut, he felt trapped.

"Good morning, Harrison," the young man stood up from his chair behind his large wooden desk, reached across it and shook Harrison's hand in greeting.

Harrison wasn't sure what he thought about having a boss younger than himself. In fact, when Harrison started with the company twenty-one years ago, Eric Meyers was starting the third grade.

"Please, have a seat," Eric offered and motioned toward the chair to Harrison's left in front of the desk. "How are you these days?" he continued.

"Fine, I guess," Harrison answered. He noticed a small stack of files in front of Eric. He recognized the handwriting on them. "What's going on?" he asked, trying to not sound too demanding but failing. "Are those my files—"

"They're the company's files," Eric corrected. He flipped the top one open and then closed it. "Harrison, I'll be blunt with you. These files are not like you at all. There are mistakes after mistakes all through them—"

"Mistakes?" Harrison interrupted and sat forward in his chair.

"Yes, mistakes." Eric took a sheet of paper from the top file. He turned it around and slid it across the desk but kept his hand on it. "Is that your signature?"

Harrison studied the document. The signature was his but the rest of the data was not. "I didn't do—"

"Is that your signature? Answer the question." Eric repeated with all of the finesse of a seasoned lawyer.

"It is, but—"

"Ut, ut," again Eric interrupted, this time holding up a halting hand. "So, I will ask you again, is everything all right?"

Harrison sat back in his chair. "I have been a little stressed these past few days."

"Stressed? About what?"

"It's not job related. It's a personal matter."

"Well," Eric said, placing the document back into the file. "You're making it a work-related matter. If Debra hadn't caught this before it was sent out to the client, we would have lost them. It would have cost the company dearly. Harrison, Global Shipping is one of this company's biggest clients. Losing them over some *personal problem* is not acceptable.

"So, I ask you again, as your friend, what is the matter?"

Friend? When did we become friends? I only see you occasionally here at work. We don't mix in the same circles. We don't socialize.

Harrison hesitated a moment to let his thoughts quiet down again.

"My renter is missing. He left for San Diego last Tuesday and never arrived."

"I see," Eric breathed and rocked back in his chair.

"I've tried going to the police but they can't help. Thomas is an adult in good health, they say. The state police said they would take the report but unless I could prove a crime has been committed or that he was in danger, they just don't have the manpower to send out a search party. I think that last part was meant to be sarcastic," Harrison said but his tone failed to express any trace of humor.

"Why does this worry you?" Eric asked.

"I don't know. He's my friend and this is not like him at all. In the past he's always phoned, emailed or texted when he was away, just to let me know he was okay. But this time, nothing. I just have a bad feeling that something has gone wrong but I can't prove it."

Eric started nodding his head. Harrison had to avoid looking at him because it reminded him of the plastic, bobble head figurine on Justus' desk in the file room downstairs. He didn't want to laugh.

"Well, I'm sorry you're going through this," Eric said in an uncommonly kind way. But then, predictably, his tone changed back to his cold, formal business one. "Normally in a situation like this it would be grounds for dismissal."

"You're firing me?"

"I should," Eric looked at Harrison. "These are serious mistakes and not just on Global's account. There's A-Boy Plumbing, Camera World, Legacy, Powell's," he read off the names as he flipped through the stack of files. "If these weren't caught it could have ruined the company."

"I see," Harrison said. Part of him was still confused. He had always been careful with his reports, checking and double, even triple checking the figures to be sure they were accurate. Plus, he hadn't worked on half of those accounts in over two weeks. Their reports weren't due yet.

You can't trust Debra. Justus' voice whispered in Harrison's head.

"You've been with the company for over twenty years," Eric continued speaking. "I really don't want to have to do this but you left me no choice."

"So, you *are* firing me." Harrison said and clenched his teeth. Part of him wanted to grab the spoiled brat and turn him over his knee but it wouldn't prove anything.

"No, not yet. In light of the circumstances, I'm suspending you without pay for two weeks, pending a final decision. In that time I suggest you get your mind focused and your head back in the game. If you can prove to me you are back one hundred percent then you may still have a job here."

Harrison nodded. The image of little third grade Eric sitting in his father's office chair, peeking over the top of the desk, flashed in his mind.

"The suspension begins immediately." Eric added. "Collect what you need from your desk and then I don't want to see or hear from you for the next two weeks."

"Okay," Harrison answered. He stood up and without saying another word, left the boss' office.

Downstairs Harrison ignored the stares from his co-workers, obviously they had all heard about his meeting upstairs. He walked straight to his cubicle where he found Justus waiting for him.

"So, how did it go?" Justus asked in a whisper.

"Suspended for two weeks," Harrison answered.

"What?" Justus raised his voice just above a whisper.

"Pending dismissal."

"Why?" Justus nearly shouted.

Harrison hushed him with a sharp look. "Eric claims I made mistakes on a bunch of accounts."

"No way! I've read your reports. I didn't see any mistakes."

Harrison looked at the file clerk in surprise. "You have?"

"When it's slow in the file room, I sometimes read over

the files before putting them away," Justus sheepishly admitted.

"Interesting. I never knew that."

"That's because I haven't told anyone, except maybe Debra and now you. The only reason Debra knows is I happened to see one of her mistakes and told her about it. She's notorious for transposing numbers."

"Is she now?" Harrison said looking in the direction of Debra's cubicle. "You don't suppose she would sabotage my reports?"

"Possibly, but what makes you think that?"

"Because some of the accounts Eric said had mistakes on them I haven't worked on in weeks. Who went through my files before I got here this morning?"

"I don't know. They were all over your desk when I arrived. I was just trying to straighten them up."

"Thanks. Well, I have to go before the boss comes down to check to make sure I'm gone and before Debra gets in. I don't want her to see me leaving if in fact she set me up."

"Okay. I'll call you tonight and let you know if I hear anything."

"Sounds good."

Not wanting to run into Debra at the elevators, Harrison took the stairs down a flight and caught the descending elevator there. The closer he got to his home in Southwest Portland, the more his problems at work faded and were replaced with the more important matter at hand, Thomas.

Col. Mustard lay perched on the back of Thomas' La-Z-Boy staring out the front window. He was not pleased to see Harrison walk through the front door early. He looked over his shoulder and cast a disapproving glare before returning to the more interesting view outside.

Harrison ignored the look and went straight to his bedroom and changed his clothes. At any other time two weeks off work would have been a welcome holiday but under the present circumstance, it felt more like a prison sentence. More time to sit idle and worry. Sitting down in front of his computer, Harrison first checked his emails. Nothing. Not even a brief note from Danika.

He pulled up his bank's website and entered Thomas' account information and password. Clicking on the Visa icon, he looked over the posted charges. There was nothing new, just the one charge for gas in Port Orford. He logged out.

Next he pulled up the Google Maps website and typed in his address and the address of Thomas' mother. After forcing the route to follow the coast highway, he began to formulate an idea and then a plan.

The rest of the day was spent printing off maps and directions, packing a suitcase, making a brief trip to the grocery store to stock up on cat food for Col. Mustard and filling up his gas tank at the ARCO Station. He straightened up the guest bedroom upstairs and then waited for Justus to phone when he got off work.

The minutes seemed to pass like hours. Harrison made another pass through the house to be sure everything was in its place and ready for his plan to be set into motion. *If only Justus would hurry up and call.*

At twenty to six there was a knock at the front door. Harrison froze mid-pace in the kitchen, not sure if he really heard what he thought he had. Another knock and he went to see who was calling. When he opened the door he was greeted by a familiar smiling face.

"I thought you said you were going to call?"

"I did but then I thought I might come over instead. I

didn't want to chance being overheard by anyone from work and I can't use the phone at my parents' because they tend to eavesdrop," Justus explained.

"Well, come on in." Harrison stepped aside and let Justus enter the foyer before closing the front door. "Would you like something to drink, water, a coke?"

"Do you have anything stronger?"

"Sure, would a glass of wine be okay?"

"Red if you have it."

"Choosy little bugger, I have white," Harrison smirked.

"Sure," Justus shrugged indifferently.

Harrison retrieved two glasses of wine from the kitchen and handed one to Justus who made himself comfortable on the sofa. Harrison sat down in Thomas' chair across from him.

"So, what happened after I left?" Harrison asked and took a sip of his wine. He let the sweet yet tart liquid swirl around his tongue before swallowing.

"Well, after you left a lot of people started talking. Some were shocked and angry. Others said some pretty interesting things. The consensus is that Debra is looking to get promoted to management by turning on her co-workers. Sam was written up for being five minutes late."

"But he's always late. It's Tri-Met's fault. Everyone knows he makes it up at the end of the day and then some."

"Yeah, well, Debra ratted him out to Eric. But that's not the half of it. She's managed to get our breaks and lunches monitored and if anyone is so much as a minute late coming back they get written up. Eric said if a person has more than five occurrences in a week, they will receive disciplinary action."

"I guess I'm glad I'm suspended for the next two weeks."

"Say, what are you going to do?" Justus asked and took a gulp from his wine glass.

"That's what I wanted to talk to you about."

CHAPTER FOUR

Of course it was raining. It never failed, especially when Harrison had something important to do and today was one of those days. Pulling the collar of his coat tighter around his neck, he dashed out the kitchen door and threw his suitcase into the back of the Bug. He slammed the hatch shut and ran back to the dry kitchen. Double checking that he had the power cords for his laptop and the charger for his phone, he zipped his messenger bag closed and dropped the flap over it.

It's a murse, Thomas' voice echoed in Harrison's ears.

A what? Harrison asked.

A murse, a man purse.

No, it's a messenger bag. Harrison corrected.

Call it whatever you want, but if it has a shoulder strap like a lady's purse, a zippered pouch, it's a murse.

Harrison smiled and shook his head at the memory.

A knock at the front door sent Harrison on his way. The clock in the foyer chimed eight. Justus was right on time. Harrison opened the door and his expression changed to surprise.

On the front porch were four boxes and Justus standing with his suitcase in hand. Behind him, his father was walking up the steps with yet another box in his hands.

"Good morning, Mr. Andrews," Justus' father greeted.

"'Morning. You can call me Harrison," Harrison replied and stepped out of the way.

"Nick," Justus' father semi-introduced himself while he moved the boxes from the porch to the foyer.

Harrison watched in shock and looked at Justus who stood with both hands holding onto the handle of his suitcase and smiling coyly.

"What's all this?" Harrison asked.

"I really want to thank you for letting Justus move in with you."

Harrison's mouth dropped open in shock. Words failed him as Nick set the last of the boxes down.

"That's it. Nice to meet you." Nick grabbed Harrison's hand and gave it a firm shake. "See ya'."

Before he could speak, Nick was out the door and down the walk. Justus closed the front door and broke the spell.

"Justus, what's all of this? What's going on?"

"Last night I sort-a told my parents you wanted me to move in."

"For a few days," Harrison clarified.

"I guess they misunderstood? They were so happy I couldn't let them down."

"But—"

"Oh my, you best be getting on the road and I need to get to work."

"You can put your things in the spare room at the top of the stairs." Harrison relented and led the way. "I set a bed up for you. There are extra blankets and sheets in the downstairs linen closet. You'll have to make do with using queen top sheets. I don't have twin sheets. There's a laundry rack for you to hang your clothes on and an old chest of drawers."

Justus looked around the small room and nodded. "This will be fine. It actually looks bigger than my old room at my parents'."

Harrison didn't hear a word. His focus was on starting his journey and there just wasn't time to get into it now. He watched Justus throw his suitcase on the bed before he turned around and led him back down the stairs to the kitchen.

"Col. Mustard gets half a can of cat food in the morning and fresh water in his bowl. Be sure to wash his bowls out every day otherwise he gets sores around his mouth. You can leave him a bowl of dry cat food to nibble on during the day. In the evening, give him the other half of the can food. Also, his cat box is in the mud room. Be sure to clean it daily or he will leave you a little surprise on your bed." *Actually my bed,* Harrison realized.

"My bedroom and Thomas' bedroom are off limits. No snooping through drawers or closets. I have stocked the fridge and freezer for you. There is also more stuff in the pantry. Here's some extra money for milk and what not. Make it last." Harrison handed an envelope to Justus. He folded it in half and tucked it into the back pocket of his Dockers.

"Do you have any questions?" Harrison hesitated to ask but had to.

"Yes, where is Col. Mustard?"

Harrison looked around the kitchen and then walked back to the living room. "He's probably hiding. He doesn't care for strangers much. He'll probably stay hidden until things quiet down. And that's another thing; he doesn't go outside, *ever.*"

"Got it!" Justus said and nodded.

"I've left you my cell number and the number of Thomas' mother. I've also forwarded the house phone to my cell, so you will want to use your cell phone for your friends and whoever else may want to reach you. I want to make sure if Thomas does call that I get it."

"Sounds good."

"Any questions?"

"Keys?"

"Oh, yes. Here." Harrison handed him the spare house key on a bright orange, spiral cord. "Don't lose it."

"Are you kidding?" he laughed and took the key. Stretching the cord, he shook his head. "This is just like what my dad put my grandmother's keys on so she wouldn't lose them."

"Alright, enough with the old people jabs. If you think of anything else, give me a call. And, if you hear any news from Thomas, call me day or night."

"Sure thing," Justus said and followed Harrison to the back door. "Could I ask you a favor? Could you drop me by work?"

"Sure get in."

After making sure the front and back doors of the house were locked, Harrison took his place in the driver's seat. While he drove, he had Justus repeat the instructions back to him.

"And no parties," Justus finished.

"Good," Harrison said.

"What if I meet someone—"

"Absolutely not!" Harrison interrupted. "You are not to bring any strangers into my house while I'm gone."

"But—"

"No!" Harrison snapped. "If you have to do that stuff

you can go to their place."

"That stuff?" Justus laughed. "You are such a prude."

"A prude? Do kids still say that?"

"No. I only hear my parents say that about their friends."

Harrison shook his head and felt old. He pulled over to the curb across from the Bank Tower and let Justus out.

"Call me when you get settled tonight," Justus said before he shut the car door.

"I will." Harrison agreed.

The rain turned to a downpour before Harrison could reach the southbound ramp to I-5. The windshield wipers on his VW Bug could scarcely keep up even on the highest setting. Traffic slowed to a near crawl which enabled Harrison to merge onto the highway with ease.

Just south of Wilsonville, the sky opened up and the clouds gave way to a beautiful sunny day. Finally, Harrison relaxed his grip on the steering wheel and sat back in his seat. Traffic lightened some and began to move. Harrison glanced at the loose sheets of paper in the passenger seat. Google Maps was wrong. It had said it would only take about an hour to reach Salem. *Guess they didn't account for the rain,* Harrison thought. Now nearly a half an hour behind schedule, Harrison wondered if he would make Ellensburg before sundown.

The cell phone rang just as Harrison passed Albany. Startled, he jumped and the VW Bug swerved. Shutting off the radio, he hit the speaker button on his phone.

"Hello?"

"Harrison?"

"Hi, Dani, what's up?"

"I just—what are you doing?"

"I'm driving. I have you on speaker."

"I can tell. I thought you would be at work and was expecting to get your voice mail."

"Yeah, well, that's a long story. The short version is, I was suspended for two weeks and—"

"Suspended? Why? What happened?"

"I don't really know. I think one of the gals at work is trying to stir things up. It's crazy and too much for me to think about right now with Thomas missing. I'm on my way to Port Orford."

"Port Orford? What on earth for?"

"I'm retracing Thomas' route to see if I can find him. His mother called the other day; he still hasn't arrived. I've checked with his friends in San Francisco and they haven't heard from him either."

"Harry, why are you doing this? I mean, why don't you let the police take care of it?"

"They won't. They told me there is no evidence of a crime and given Thomas' age and health, there is no reason for concern that he is in physical danger, blah, blah, blah."

"I get that," Danika answered.

There was silence for what felt like a long time.

"You still there?" Harrison asked.

"Yes," Danika answered. "I was just thinking."

"About what?"

"About—Harry, why are you doing this?"

"I told you, the police—"

"No, I mean, after mom and dad died, you put your life on hold to look after me."

"Yeah, what's that got to do with anything?"

"When did you meet Thomas?"

"About eight years ago."

"Right after I got married."

"So."

"Don't you see, you found someone else to mother."

"No, I didn't."

"What are you doing now?"

There was a long pause while Harrison let her words sink in.

"But, he's my friend, Dani. I'm worried about him."

"I know," Danika's tone relaxed. "I would probably do the same thing. Just promise me you'll be careful."

"I promise."

"And check in with me every night. Call, text or email. I don't care if you're three hours behind me; I want to know what's going on."

"I will," Harrison promised. "Hey, what's up? Why'd you call? Is everything okay there?"

"Everything's great." Harrison could hear the smile in her tone. "I just wanted you to be the first to hear the news. I got the promotion. I'm an Assistant D.A."

"Dani, that's fantastic. Congratulations. When do you start?"

"In two weeks."

"That's wonderful. Oh," Harrison's tone dropped. "I suppose that means you and the boys won't be able to come out this summer."

"I'm sorry. I won't have any vacation time for six months and then we'll be starting the new school year. Robert doesn't like taking the boys out of school."

"Robert doesn't like a lot of things." Harrison muttered.

"What? You're starting to break up."

"I guess I'll let you go. I'll call you tonight. Congrats on the job. Love you."

"Love you, too."

The connection went dead before Harrison had a chance to hang up.

Turning off I-5 at Drain and heading west toward Reedsport on the coast, Harrison's mind kept going over what Danika had said. After their parents died Harrison did step up to be not only brother but mother and father to Danika. She was only twelve and needed him. Thomas was twenty-three when he moved in. The last thing he needed was to be parented. *No, she's wrong,* Harrison reassured himself.

Highway 101 south was a beautiful drive. Tall green fir trees lined long stretches of the mostly two-lane highway. Harrison glanced at his watch. It was well past lunchtime and his stomach was beginning to growl at him. When he reached Coos Bay he pulled into the McDonald's. He found a parking space close to the doors. It felt good to get out and stretch his legs. He hadn't realized he had been driving for four and a half hours without stopping. Searching the menu screens, he settled on breakfast and placed his order to-go. Port Orford was only an hour away and he was anxious to get there. However, eating and sipping on his Coke would be a nice distraction that would help the miles pass quickly.

The traffic speed slowed just outside the town's limits. *Town, that was a generous word,* Harrison smiled to himself. From what he could see, Port Orford consisted of a bunch of old worn out buildings that looked abandoned, a couple gas stations, a church whose steeple resembled a lighthouse and a Ray's grocery store. It seemed to him this was not a destination town but one people just passed through on their way to someplace more exciting.

Harrison's stomach began to grumble again, mostly from nerves. *Perhaps a breakfast burrito hadn't been the best choice.* He drove slower, searching for a sign for Hank's Gas

Station. *Thomas would have stayed on the highway. He wouldn't have ventured onto the side streets. It must be here.* Then, he spotted it. A makeshift sign painted on a large sheet of plywood bolted to a pole. *Thomas stopped here?* The place gave Harrison the creeps. It reminded him of those last-chance-for-gas gas stations in old slasher movies. Still, he pulled his Bug up to the pumps and shut off the engine.

A young man came out of a small garage set back on the lot away from the pumps. In his blue Dockers and a dingy white shirt, he was every bit the scary attendant from those movies.

The man took a final drag from his cigarette before tossing it to the ground and crushing it out with the toe of his logger boot. He walked over to the driver side window, adjusted his baseball cap and asked, "What can I do for you?" His voice was hoarse. He was pleasant looking enough, sandy blonde hair, blue eyes, scruffy two-day old stubble, but his teeth were stained from his smoking.

"Fill it with regular unleaded," Harrison answered and handed him his credit card. Once the man moved away from the door, Harrison opened it and stepped out.

"Nice ride," the attendant commented and handed Harrison back his card. "Get good mileage with these."

It sounded more like a statement than a question.

"It does pretty good," Harrison answered.

"Bet it rides like a go-cart," the man gave a little chuckle.

"Sometimes it feels like one," Harrison answered and tugged on his earlobe. He wasn't into making small-talk with strangers but knew he needed to warm him up before he asked his questions. "Bet you see a lot of cars pass through here."

The attendant looked at him. "Yep. See 'em all. Junkers

to cherries."

"Say, you wouldn't happen to have been working a week ago last Tuesday would you?" Harrison went for it with a bit of trepidation.

"Work here every day, all day," he answered.

Harrison pulled out the two photographs from his shirt pocket.

"I was wondering if you remember seeing this man?" He held up the photo of Thomas.

The attendant gave it a glance and shook his head. "Nope."

Harrison held up the second photo, the one of Thomas and his Cadillac.

"He was driving this."

This time the attendant took a longer look and started nodding. Harrison felt hopeful.

"Sweet! A classic Deville." Then he shook his head. "Nope. Didn't see it neither. You a cop?"

"No," Harrison nearly laughed. "I'm just looking for my friend. He stopped here and bought gas. Then it's like he just vanished."

"Wow. Sorry about that. Wish I could be more help but I didn't see him," he said and shook his head. He sounded sincere but Harrison thought it odd how he avoided eye contact.

"No problem. Say, is there a restroom I can use?"

"Sure, the key is on a stick just inside the office door. The john is around back. Make sure you lock it when you leave. Don't want none of those little brats from across the way getting in there and making a mess."

"Thanks."

Harrison tried not to look too desperate but hurried none

the less. With the key in hand, he made his way around the side of the garage. A yellow arrow and the word restroom were sloppily painted on the seven foot tall wooden fence that ran the width of the property and directed him behind the building. The fence created a narrow alleyway behind the garage. The restroom door was located in the center of the wall. From the smell in the air, Harrison guessed some people didn't bother with the key, let alone the restroom, and did their business on the side of the building or fence instead. Harrison unlocked the restroom door and opened it. Immediately he took a step back and choked, gasping for fresh air. *Or maybe they preferred the outside air over the stench in the restroom,* Harrison thought.

Harrison's need for relief overruled his sense of smell. He buried his nose in the crook of his arm and went inside. Using the one-foot, wooden stick chained to the key, he propped the door open. He quickly unzipped in front of the urinal. Holding his breath as long as he could, he finally felt some much needed relief. Zipping up, he took one look at the black grease stained and soiled sink and decided his hands were cleaner without washing. Besides, he had hand sanitizer back in his car.

After putting the key back in the office, Harrison returned to his car. The attendant suddenly stood up beside the front left tire.

"You're finished?" he announced, though it sounded more like a question than a statement.

"Yes, thank you. I can honestly say that I've never seen a restroom quite like yours."

"Good," he smiled and bobbed his head.

What a doofus, Harrison thought.

"You're all good to go." He returned the nozzle to the pump and tightened the gas cap before handing Harrison his receipt.

Harrison tucked it into his shirt pocket. Something about the attendant made him feel uneasy. He'd look at the receipt later.

Back in the safety of his Bug, Harrison started the engine and pulled back onto the highway. According to Google Maps, he was only a half an hour north of Ellensburg. He would make it just about sundown.

South of town the highway began to climb. Fir trees hid the slope of the hillside on the left; while on the right, evergreen shrubs and smaller trees along the roadside framed the beautiful view of the Pacific Ocean. *I see why Thomas likes this route.*

Without warning, the engine began to chug. Harrison gripped the wheel a bit tighter and eased up on the gas. He checked his gauges and they all appeared to be normal.

"Sorry, ol' boy. Cheap gas. If you will just hang in there until Ellensburg I'll see if I can do you better," he said aloud and patted the dashboard.

Once he reached the top of the rise the knocking quit and the Bug rode smoothly again.

A few miles later, with the sun beginning to near the horizon, Harrison turned away from the ocean and headed inland around Humbug Mountain. *Strange name.* He made a note to Google it when he reached Ellensburg to find out where it got its name.

Once around the tight turns the highway headed back toward the ocean. A thought occurred to Harrison. Since leaving Port Orford he hadn't seen a single car in the oncoming lane.

One more turn and he slammed on the brakes. The Bug swerved and the tires squealed as it came to a stop. Harrison's heart beat faster. In front of him was a road crew working on a section of the highway that had broken away and sunk. A brave man holding a stop sign stood in front of the line of stopped cars. Slowly cars in the oncoming lane began to pass by.

Harrison looked out his window at the ocean. The edges of the sun had begun to dip into the waters of the Pacific turning the blue sky into vivid shades of pinks and oranges.

Well, if I had to be stuck somewhere, at least I have a nice view of the sunset.

Harrison checked to be sure his headlights were on just as the flagger flipped his sign to "Slow" and motioned for them all to move over into the oncoming lane. The heap in front of him chugged and expelled a cloud of black exhaust. The fumes seeped their way into Harrison's Bug. He coughed and cursed the driver under his breath.

I'll never complain about the DEQ in Portland again. At least we don't have junkers like that driving around the streets polluting the air back home.

Harrison held back, letting the other cars pass him while he continued along the highway. Soon, they were nowhere in sight and he was once again alone on the road. He felt his shoulders relax. He pulled out a cd and slipped it into the player. Belinda Carlisle serenaded him while he continued south along the highway.

Just when he came to a hill, the sun slipped below the horizon. The car suddenly gave a violent shimmy and backfired. Harrison shut the stereo off and gripped the wheel tighter.

"What the matter ol' boy?" He again started talking to his car.

He noticed a turn out ahead and willed his Bug to make

it at least that far. The check oil light came on.

"What the—" Suddenly he saw the face of the gas attendant flash in his mind. He remembered seeing him stand up quickly beside his front tire. The car shimmied again. "It's just a few more feet. I promise," he said aloud patting his dashboard.

Once he crested the hill the road turned to the left but on the right was a viewpoint turn-out for people to take in what he assumed was a spectacular view. Harrison turned the steering wheel right and gently eased the VW off the highway and onto the graveled shoulder. Applying the brakes he could feel the gravel slipping under his tires and heard it pelting the underside of the wheel wells. Pushing harder, the car finally came to a stop. The headlights shone on a street sign, "Ellensburg 1 mile".

Harrison shut the engine off and slumped over the wheel for a moment while he thought about what to do. He pulled out his cell phone and held it up.

"Damn!" he muttered when he saw there wasn't a signal. He tossed his useless phone aside and switched on the emergency flashers. Looking out at the view he decided to get some fresh air.

The slight breeze felt cold and damp against his cheeks. Walking around to the passenger side he leaned against his Bug. The darkness of night chased the lingering glow of the day across the sky until any trace of the sun was erased. Across the bay, toward the south, tiny dots of light flickered on the shore like fallen stars.

"So close and yet—"

The sound of a truck approaching from the north interrupted Harrison's thoughts. He stood up and turned to face the sound. Two headlights drew nearer. Harrison could hear the engine shift down and knew the truck was slowing. He walked back around to the driver's door and stood ready to jump back into his car at the first sign of trouble.

The truck, a utility pick-up with a cherry picker bucket on the back, slowed. In the blinking light of the VW's emergency flashers, Harrison made out the lettering on the side of the truck as it passed. *Charter* was emblazoned on the passenger door along with a telephone number and company logo that resembled a window with a breeze blowing through it. The driver pulled off the highway and stopped just a few feet in front of Harrison's VW.

Harrison's heart began to beat faster. He cursed himself for watching those old slasher movies from the 1990's because now every scene played in his mind. The driver left the truck running and opened the door. The cab light came on but Harrison couldn't see much due to the bucket on the cherry picker blocking most of his view. The crunching sound of footsteps on gravel warned him that the driver was coming toward him. Harrison put his hand on the door handle, ready to jump back into the seeming safety of his car at the first sight of an axe or machete or fisherman's gaff.

The driver stopped when he reached the end of his truck bed. Standing beside the red tail lights, he squinted at the yellow pulsating glow of Harrison's emergency flashers.

"Having a bit of trouble?" the driver asked. His voice was deep but non-threatening.

"Yes," Harrison answered.

"What seems to be the trouble?" The man started to walk toward Harrison but Harrison didn't feel afraid. After all, the monsters in the movies all sounded menacing. This guy sounded, normal.

"The check oil light came on. Are you from around

here?"

"Not originally, but I am now," the man answered sounding almost proud. He looked at Harrison and cocked his head slightly. "Say, don't I know you?"

"I don't think so. I'm from Portland," Harrison answered and felt a little uncomfortable with the way the man was looking him over.

"That's where I'm from originally. What's your name?"

"Harrison—"

"Andrews," the driver added. "I knew it! Harrison Andrews," he repeated. "Of all the people to run into and here of all places. What's it been? Sixteen years since high school?"

"Twenty-three to be exact."

"Twenty-three? Sheesh, where did the time go?"

Harrison was beginning to feel a bit creeped out. He tried to remember the people he hung out with back in the day who would be living this far from Portland but no one was coming to mind. In the darkening light and the glow from the red and yellow lights it was hard to distinguish the man's features clearly.

The driver let out a laugh. "Still don't recognize me?" he said and pulled out a flashlight, switched it on and turned the light on himself.

Harrison immediately jumped. The harsh light cast dark shadows across the man's face and only made him look more like the killers in the movies than anyone he could recognize.

"It's me, Douglas—"

"Doug Blair?" Harrison suddenly recognized him. How could he have forgotten his childhood best friend? "What are you doing down here?"

"Working for the telephone company and fishing. Well, mostly working, really."

"Wow!" Harrison couldn't believe his luck.

"What are you doing down here at this hour?"

"It's a long story but I was heading into Ellensburg for the night when my car decided to die on me."

"I'm sorry about your car but this is crazy. You have reservations in town?"

"No. I was just going to see if they have a Best Western and—"

"Say no more, you're spending the night with my wife and me."

"You're married?"

"Going on...a long time now," Douglas laughed heartily.

"I don't know," Harrison hesitated.

"Nonsense, we can catch up on the last twenty-three years, you say?"

"Yes."

"Grab your stuff. We can leave your car here until morning."

"But is it safe?"

"We can move it over there and it'll be fine." He motioned toward the guardrail away from the road. "Hardly anyone travels this highway at night."

CHAPTER FIVE

Moments later, Harrison was perched in the passenger seat of Douglas' Charter truck with his laptop and suitcase resting on his lap. Every once and again, he would steal a look of his old friend and try to connect the images of the boy from his memory to the man beside him. It was proving harder than it should but it could have been due to the dim light.

"Good grief," Douglas said and shook his head. "The last time I saw you was just after graduation. We were supposed to go to Oregon State together, remember?"

"Yes." Harrison did remember.

"What happened again?"

"My mother died."

"Oh that's right. A car accident?"

"No, cancer."

"That's rough. I'm so sorry."

Harrison could hear the uneasiness in Douglas' tone and knew this line of conversation was uncomfortable for him.

"What about you? Did you graduate?"

"Nah," Douglas shrugged. "I had to drop out after my

sophomore year." He shook his head. "My girlfriend told me she was pregnant. Her parents insisted we get married. I thought I was in love, so we did."

"So you have a kid?"

"Nope. She faked the whole thing. She was never really pregnant."

"Oh no," Harrison breathed. "What did you do?"

"I divorced the bitch," Douglas spat. "Our marriage was based on a lie. Oh, I tried to be forgiving and stick it out but I couldn't do it. I felt deceived and every time I looked at her I felt resentful. How was I supposed to trust her after that?"

"I'm sorry."

"What about you? You married?" Douglas redirected the conversation.

"No. After my mother died, my father started drinking and ended up dying a year and a half later. I had to go to work and look after my sister."

"That's right! You have a sister. What's her name? Da-Dan-Danielle?"

"Danika. We, I, I call her Dani."

"Dani." Douglas shook his head. "She was a cute little thing. I remember she always wanted to tag along with us to the football games."

"Yeah," Harrison smiled at the memory.

"Whatever happened to her?"

"She went to OSU and then to law school. She moved to Virginia and is now an assistant D.A.."

"Good for her! She married?"

"Yeah," Harrison said and let out a sigh.

"Uh-oh, you don't like him?"

"I did at first but he's a jerk. He's the Chief of Police there and he's also abusive. I worry about Dani and the boys."

"Oh, so she's got kids?"

"Two, two boys, seven and five."

"Sounds nice. So, why haven't you married?"

Harrison shook his head. "I don't know. I guess I'm just waiting for the right person to come along. But you married again?"

"Yep. Before I moved down here I met a really nice gal. Well, actually, I had an accident on my motorcycle and she was the EMT who came to my rescue." Douglas chuckled.

While they talked Harrison was trying to keep track of the route they were going. Once they left the viewpoint, Douglas continued along the highway, down the hill toward the lights that Harrison saw across the bay. When they reached a bridge, Douglas took a sharp turn left and headed away from the ocean and the lights.

The road twisted and turned several times until Harrison could no longer distinguish east from west or north from south. In the darkness he could make out tall fir trees on either side of the road and a few rural mailboxes on posts but little else.

"Almost there," Douglas announced.

He slowed and turned off the paved road onto a narrow gravel drive. The trees and shrubs had been cleared away from both sides of the road. Ahead on the right, in the beams of the headlights, Harrison made out what looked like two telephone poles closer together than normal. There was another pole resting on top of them like a cross beam. As they neared the structure, Douglas slowed. Harrison saw a gravel driveway and realized the structure was a rustic gate. A wooden sign hung down on chains in the center of the beam. It read, Blair Ranch.

"You live on a ranch?" Harrison asked.

Douglas let out a laugh. "Nah, we just have a bunch of chickens. Blair Ranch just sounded better than Blair House."

Douglas slowed the truck even more and followed the long drive as it bent to the right and then to the left. Harrison couldn't see much through the side windows. When they rounded a turn to the right, a large log house came into view.

"Nice," Harrison breathed.

"It is now but it was a pain building."

"You built that?" Harrison didn't try to hide the surprise in his tone.

"Yep. The outside went up pretty fast but it took a few years until we finished the inside to our liking." He pulled the truck up to a log which separated the driveway from the front lawn.

Harrison climbed down out of the truck and took a closer look at the house. A covered porch stretched the entire width of the front of the log house. Three steps led to the center of the porch and to the front door. The lights were on inside and illuminated the large window on the right. The window on the left was dark.

While Harrison walked across the porch he couldn't help but be impressed. The porch felt solid, no creaking or give. It was a far cry from the forts they built as boys.

"Come on in and meet my wife," Douglas said. "You're gonna like her."

"Okay," Harrison answered. He still wasn't sure about spending the night with them. Even though they had gone through elementary, middle and high school together and were best friends, the time apart had made them practically strangers. Harrison tried to find the old feelings of closeness they once shared but they were buried deep inside.

"Barb," Douglas called out when he opened the front door. "We've got company."

Harrison was sure that last part sounded like a warning.

He listened for a reply.

Just inside the front door a flight of wooden stairs rose to the second floor. A rough, twisted section of log served as a support for the thinner, gnarled, tree branches that were used for a handrail and banister. While Harrison stood looking at the landing at the top, a woman walked out of what he assumed was a bedroom. She was a pleasant looking, her short blonde hair was pulled back in a ponytail, she wore a white uniform blouse with EMT patches sewn on the short sleeves and over one breast, a badge and name tag were pinned on the other.

"Hi," she greeted Harrison with a smile that immediately faded when she looked at her husband.

"Barbara, I'd like you to meet my best friend from my school days, Harrison. He had a bit of car trouble at the viewpoint. I've invited him to spend the night."

"Fine with me, I've been called into work."

"You have?" Douglas groaned. "Not again."

"What can I say?" Barbara shook her head and shrugged her shoulders. "I've left our dinner in the oven, lasagna. There is plenty for the two of you. You'll have to straighten up the guest room. If I had some warning, I would have done it. There are some fresh towels in the closet. I have to go." She gave Douglas a brief kiss and then smiled at Harrison. "Pleased to meet you. I'm sure I'll see you in the morning." She held out her hand.

"Nice to meet you as well," he answered and gave her hand a gentle shake.

Before another word was spoken, Barbara grabbed her purse, jacket and keys from the closet beside the front door and was gone.

"Well, looks like it's just the two of us tonight,"

Douglas said. "Just put your stuff down. Let's eat."

Harrison looked around and set his suitcase on the floor by the end of the sofa that was set against the staircase wall. He put his laptop case on the sofa. Taking a quick glance at his phone, he was relieved to see he had service once again.

"What would you like to drink? I have beer and beer?" Douglas called from the kitchen on the other side of the living room wall.

"Beer would be great," Harrison answered even though he really didn't care for the stuff. He walked across the small living room to where a round dining table sat under a stained glass chandelier. Three large, six foot by six foot windows lined the outer wall, two in the living room, one in the dining room. It was too dark for Harrison to see what sort of view they offered. Instead he turned toward the kitchen.

Douglas was bent down taking out a large pan of lasagna out of the oven. He held it up in his mitted hands and took a deep breath.

"You're in for a real treat, my friend," he said grinning. "Barbara is famous for her lasagna. When she makes it, she makes a ton of it because it's even good cold."

"Smells wonderful," Harrison complimented and took in a slow, deep breath, savoring the aroma. Lasagna was his favorite.

Douglas brought the pan over to the table and set it down on the trivet in the center. He removed his gloves and rushed back into the kitchen where he closed the oven, grabbed two bottles of beer from the fridge, plates and a couple forks.

"Oh, almost forgot," he said setting his load down on the table and returning to the kitchen. "Can't have lasagna without fresh garlic bread."

The two sat down and began to eat. Harrison was pleasantly surprised by just how good the lasagna tasted. Douglas hadn't exaggerated.

"So, you were saying it was a long story how you ended up down here?" Douglas renewed their conversation.

"Yeah," Harrison nodded.

"Well, looks like it's just you and me and we have all night, so tell me about it."

"I'm looking for my boarder."

"Boarder?" Douglas scrunched up his nose and brow, giving Harrison a curious look.

"I rent out a room of my parents' house to a friend," he explained. "Last Tuesday, Thomas headed off to see his mother in San Diego, but he never made it."

"Have you gone to the police?"

"Oh yes. The policewoman in Portland and the State Police said the same thing. Since Thomas doesn't have a medical condition and I have no reason to believe he is a danger to himself or that a crime has been committed, there is little they can do. At least the State Police took a report but they aren't actively searching for him."

"Sounds a lot like the worthless police we have here in town. Another beer?" Douglas offered and stood up. Not waiting for Harrison to answer, he retrieved two more bottles from the refrigerator.

"Thanks," Harrison said and looked at the new bottle.

"So, since the police weren't much help, what happened next?"

"I decided to start looking on my own."

"I see." Douglas nodded and took a large drink from his bottle and then belched.

"According to Thomas' bank records, the last place he

used his credit card was at Hanks' Gas Station in Port Orford." Harrison continued. "But when I stopped there this afternoon, the guy there said he didn't recognize Thomas or his car. He said he works there seven days a week, so he's either not very observant or he's lying."

"I think a little of both," Douglas spoke up.

"You do? You know him?"

"Oh yes," Douglas said nodding his head. He took another drink of his beer and then sat forward, resting his elbows on the table. "Bubba, everyone around here calls him that but his real name is Judd Hanks Junior. He's the oldest of the Hanks boys and the brightest but that's not saying much. Their father, Judd Hanks Senior, is the Police Chief across the river in Ellensburg. He's about as worthless as his sons.

"All those stories you hear about small town hillbillies are based on the Hanks. I swear. Gospel truth." Douglas took another drink, emptying his bottle. "Grab you another?"

"I'm good," Harrison answered and picked up his first bottle and swallowed the rest of its contents. He shuddered and set the empty aside. He opened the second bottle and set it by his plate.

"So, what's your plan now?" Douglas asked returning to his chair.

"I don't know. I guess first I'll need to find someplace to get my car fixed. Do you know of anywhere?"

Douglas shook his head. "No one I would trust here in town. I always take my vehicles to Brookings. They have a trustworthy mechanic there."

"My car won't make it. The check oil light is already on and ever since I filled up at Hanks, it's been handling strangely."

"Well, I have a hitch, I can tow you tomorrow. It may

take them a day or two to get to it, but if you don't mind staying here…"

"Are you sure your wife won't mind?" Harrison hesitated.

"No, she's an angel. She'll be fine with it."

After clearing the table and putting the dirty dishes in the dishwasher, the two men moved back into the living room. Douglas continued to drink bottle after bottle of beer while Harrison nursed his second one.

CHAPTER SIX

Harrison was awakened by the sound of his cell phone ringing. Still half asleep he opened his eyes and bolted straight up in the bed. It took a minute for his brain to catch up and remind him of where he was and what happened the night before.

He grabbed his cell phone from the small bedside table and looked at the display. Danika. He answered it.

"Harrison?" her voice sounded uncertain and worried.

"Hey, Dani," he answered.

"What happened to you? You were supposed to call me when you got to your room."

"I'm sorry," he said and then launched into filling her in about all that happened the evening before. "So, it just slipped my mind."

"It's okay. I'm glad you ran into Doug. What are the odds?" she said sounding a bit more relaxed and at ease. "Well, I just had a second. Call me tonight and let me know how things go with your car. Don't forget!"

"I won't," Harrison answered and yawned. When he

hung up the call he became aware that he had a headache. *I knew there was a reason why I hate beer,* he muttered under his breath.

After getting dressed and straightening the bed, Harrison ventured out to the kitchen where he heard voices. The delicious aroma of pancakes and sausage mixed with that of freshly brewed coffee made Harrison's mouth water and his stomach growl to life.

"Good morning," Barbara smiled at him from her seat at the table. "Coffee?"

"Sure, that would be great," Harrison answered.

"You look like shit," Douglas said with a laugh.

"Thanks, and my head feels like someone hit it with a sledge hammer."

"Need something for it?" Barbara asked when she returned to the table with a steaming cup of black coffee and a small pitcher of creamer.

"No, this will do just fine. Thank you." Harrison answered and took a sip from his cup. He savored the flavor before swallowing it.

"Was that your phone I heard ringing?" Barbara asked from the kitchen. She dished up a plate of scrambled eggs and sausages along with two large, steaming, pancakes. She returned to the table and set the plate in front of Harrison.

"Thank you. It all looks great. And, yes, it was my phone. I forgot to call my sister, Dani, last night."

"Dani," Douglas said and smiled. "How is she?"

"She's fine. A bit worried about me but okay. She told me to tell you, hi. She couldn't believe that we ran into each other. Guess we should buy a lottery ticket or something."

They all laughed.

"Where does your sister live?" Barbara asked.

"She's back east in Virginia. She just got a promotion to Assistant D.A."

"That's fantastic," Barbara said and smiled. "Bet you're proud."

"A little. So how was work last night for you?" Harrison switched the direction of the conversation.

"Oh, not too bad. We responded to a call for help at the construction site on 101 just north of here. Someone got a bit impatient and decided to run past the flagger. He hit head on into the dump truck carrying gravel. He wasn't hurt too badly but he won't be driving that BMW anytime soon.

"Other than that, the night was pretty quiet." Barbara finished. "Doug was just telling me about your friend. How awful. Do you have any idea where he could be?"

"No, not really. I was going to check out the hotels in town to see if anyone has seen him or his car. Then I was going to try Brooking and on down the coast to San Diego."

"That's a lot of places to check out," Douglas said.

"Ellensburg and Brookings aren't so bad. Even Crescent City, but the closer to San Francisco the more options there are and the more side roads there are. That's a lot for one person," Barbara added.

"I have to try something. I just can't sit around and do nothing." Harrison looked at the coffee in his cup.

Barbara reached across the table and patted the back of his hand. "Sounds like you really care about your friend."

"Yeah, I do. He's like a little brother." Harrison nodded. He felt his throat begin to tighten and looked at the plate of food in front of him.

"Well, have something to eat. I'm going to get some sleep. Maybe we could go out for dinner tonight," Barbara hinted and looked at Douglas.

"Sure, why not," Douglas agreed. He gave her a quick peck on the cheek and watched her head upstairs.

"What do you say after you finish your breakfast we go get your car and tow it down to my mechanic in Brookings?" Douglas suggested.

"Sounds like a plan."

A few minutes later, with a full and contented stomach, Harrison climbed into the cab of Douglas's work truck. The two set off for the viewpoint.

With the benefit of daylight, Harrison was able to see the view while Douglas focused his attention on the road. They weren't as far off the paved road as Harrison thought the night before and the paved road was a smooth two-lane street that followed a river back to the bridge. Douglas took a right and headed up the hill toward the viewpoint.

"I really appreciate all of this," Harrison said. "But don't you have to go to work today?"

"Nah, I'm on call mostly. There aren't a whole lot of repairs or installs these days. A lot of it has been automated. I'm just here for the things that take a hands-on touch, a downed line or drop wire, a cut cable and the activations they can't do from the office. We're fine."

"Wow."

Just then they crested the hill and Douglas turned off the paved highway and onto the gravel of the lookout.

"What the—" Douglas said.

"Where is it?" Harrison gasped and felt his whole body begin to panic. "Someone stole my car?"

"Don't freak out just yet," Douglas tried to calm him. He pulled to a stop and the two men climbed out of the cab.

Harrison ran to where he had left his Bug. He looked at the ground for signs of tire tracks. With the amount of tourists that stopped to take in the view it was impossible to tell which belonged to his VW.

He felt his throat tighten and tears of frustration well up behind his eyes. He walked over to the guard rail. Normally being this high up would freak him out but his mind was preoccupied with thoughts about who would have done this. *Surely they would have seen the check oil light. They wouldn't have gone far,* he tried to convince himself.

The sunlight reflected off a rectangular piece of metal stuck in a shrub about five feet over the edge. Harrison held fast to the guardrail and leaned forward to see if he could make out what it was.

"See something?" Douglas walked up behind him.

Harrison gave a start and nearly lost his footing.

"Whoa there," Douglas chuckled and grabbed hold of Harrison's arm. "I didn't mean to startle you. What's down there?"

"Don't know," Harrison answered. "Some piece of metal stuck in a bush. From what I can tell, it looks like a license plate."

"Let me get a rope and we'll check it out."

Douglas retrieved a heavy climbing rope from a compartment on the side of his truck. He tied one end of the rope around the guardrail, thread the other end through a climbing harness he had on and tossed the rest of the rope over the side.

"Be right back," he said.

Harrison watched while Douglas lowered himself down to the bush. He plucked the license plate from the branches and held it up for Harrison to see.

"You were right. It's an Oregon plate," he announced. Before ascending back to the lookout, Douglas took a glance around. "Hang on," he called up to Harrison.

When Douglas finally came back up, his shirt was bulging with several other license plates. He sat down on the gravel and leaned his back against the guardrail support post. Then he began to go through the plates like someone dealing a deck of cards.

"We have one from Washington, California, ah, here's one from Florida," he read off.

"Wait!" Harrison gasped and took an Oregon plate from Douglas.

"What's the matter?" Douglas asked.

"This is Thomas' plate."

"Are you sure?"

"Yes, here, look." Harrison pulled the photo of Thomas' Cadillac from the breast pocket of his shirt. He held it up next to the license plate and showed them to Douglas.

Douglas examined both and his mouth dropped open. "Why would he throw his plates away?"

"He wouldn't. He paid for a custom plate," Harrison said and shook his head in disbelief. "Something has happened to him, I just know it."

"Well, first things first," Douglas said and stood up. He dusted the ground off his seat. "We need to file a police report about your missing car. Then we can deal with this." He nodded at the plate.

Once the rope and harness were safely stowed back in their compartment, Harrison and Douglas climbed back into the cab and headed for Ellensburg.

"We'll first go to the police department," Douglas said while he drove down the hill.

At the bottom of the hill they followed the road as it bent to the right and headed across an old bridge. Harrison read the small green sign, Rogue River. Once across the bridge the road again bent right and followed the side of a hill around to the opposite side. There it rose slightly and leveled off.

Like so many of the other little towns Harrison had passed through, Ellensburg seemed to be built along the sides of the highway with the taller buildings up front and smaller buildings and houses behind. They passed a two-story building on the right that had a giant wave painted on its façade. Harrison thought it looked like a tidal wave and that it was an odd thing to greet tourists. They crossed a street named Gauntlett and on the left was another two-story building. It was unmistakably the courthouse. They continued south and a couple blocks later passed a restaurant on the right, then a school and grocery store. The town appeared to be bigger than Harrison had first thought. A little further and Douglas turned off the highway and into the parking lot of a single story building. The building was painted blue-grey with a darker blue, tiled roof. A sign above the entrance simply read, Police.

"Let's go," Douglas said after parking the truck.

The two walked into the main lobby. Across from the door was a chest-high counter. A sheet of what Harrison assumed was bulletproof glass was affixed to the ceiling and the top of the counter, forming a barrier. Along the glass wall about a foot up from the counter were three metal circles that allowed safe communication. Harrison stepped up to the one in the center. He tried not to stare at the woman seated at her desk behind the glass. She continued to type on her computer and seemingly was not in any hurry to assist him. Finally after about five minutes of standing and waiting, she looked up and gave a less than enthused smile. She walked over to the glass.

"How may I help you?" Her tone matched her smile.

"I'm here to report a stolen car," Harrison answered.

"I see. Just a moment," the woman sighed and walked back to her desk and opened a drawer. She took out a large sheet of paper and returned to the window.

"What's your address?" she began.

"Well, I'm actually not from around here," Harrison said.

"His car was taken from the viewpoint across river," Douglas blurted.

"The viewpoint?" she shrieked. She took the form and made a show of tearing it in half before crumbling it up. "That's out of our jurisdiction," she snapped and glared at them. "You'll need to file that with the county." She turned and raised her left hand and pointed north. "Just go—"

"I know where it is," Douglas interrupted sounding a bit curt. "Come on. Sheriff Frank Porter's an old friend. I'm sure he'll help us out."

The two climbed back into the truck and headed back the way they came. When they reached Gauntlett Street, Douglas turned right and parked across from the south side of the courthouse building.

Douglas hesitated for a moment and looked around the cab. "Damn!" he cursed at himself.

"What's wrong?"

"Steel toe boots and they have a metal detector."

"Oh." Harrison commented.

"Well, I guess it's their problem. Let's go."

Getting past the guard stationed inside the courthouse doors was a bit of an inconvenience but not a major obstacle. The guard, an older deputy, was extremely helpful and pointed the way to the Sheriff's office.

When Harrison walked into the room he was surprised to find there wasn't any safety glass between the public and deputies. Instead there was just a chest high counter. Behind it, a man in a heavy, black, uniform shirt with patches on both shoulders and a badge above the left breast pocket looked up from his paperwork. His head was shaved but he had a dark brown mustache and goatee. He watched Harrison approach.

"What can I do for you?" he asked in a pleasant but very businesslike tone.

"I'd like to report a stolen car," Harrison answered.

"Where was this car?"

"At the viewpoint just north of town," Douglas chimed in.

"I see," the deputy said. "What makes you think it was stolen?"

"I broke down last night and left it there. When I came back this morning, it was gone."

"Have you checked with the impound yards? It might have been towed."

"Why would they tow it?" Douglas asked. "I've seen cars up and down Highway 101 that have been sitting there for weeks."

The deputy raised his eyebrow and looked at Douglas with unmistakable annoyance. He pulled a sheet of paper out from beneath the counter without looking and slapped it down on the countertop.

"We use several towing companies," he said and began to draw circles on the list. "Before we jump to conclusions, I suggest you check with these places first. If they don't have it, then come back and we'll take a report. I have to tell you, with budget cuts due to the failure of the citizens of this wonderful county to approve a bond measure, we no longer pursue stolen cars."

"What?" Douglas gasped obviously not buying the

deputy's explanation.

"You get what you pay for. Have a nice day." The deputy feigned a smile and then looked past the two men.

Outside the courthouse Harrison finally looked at the paper.

"They use towing companies from Port Orford all the way to Brookings. There are twenty-five of them," Harrison groaned.

"Don't worry. I'll help you do some calling when we get back to the house."

While Douglas drove back to the house, Harrison looked out the window only this time the scenery wasn't exciting and new. He hated the sight of every shop, every building, every street sign and even the name, Ellensburg.

When they walked back into the house, Barbara was awake and cleaning the kitchen. She looked at the forlorn expressions on their faces and dried her hands on a small towel.

"I take it, things didn't go well?" she asked.

"No. Harrison's car was stolen or towed."

"What?" Barbara gasped. She gave Harrison a sympathetic frown. "Did you go to the police?"

"Yeah, and we got the usual run-around," Douglas answered. "The city says go to the county. The county won't do anything because they're upset their bond measure didn't pass so they aren't going to do anything. The jerk wouldn't even take a report. He said we need to call the towing companies to see if they towed it first."

"Don't they have records of the cars they've had towed?"

Douglas gave her a blank look. Harrison looked at the paper in his hand and couldn't believe he didn't think of that.

"Oh well, I might as well start calling," Harrison said.

"Why don't you give me some of those numbers," Barbara said. "I can do some calling too. Between the three of us we should be able to get it done in no time."

Harrison divided up the list and gave them the information about the make, model and license plate number of his car. They sat down at the table and took out their cell phones.

Harrison dialed the first number on his list.

"Hanks' Towing," a man's voice answered.

A jolt ran through Harrison's body. He recognized that voice. It was the gas attendant in Port Orford.

"Hello?" the man said.

"Yes," Harrison found his voice. "I'm calling to see if you towed a 2002, white, Volkswagen Beetle last night. It's license plate number is 816 HUF."

"Where was it?"

"It was broke down at the viewpoint just north of Ellensburg."

"Nope," the man answered sharply.

"Are you sure?" Harrison asked.

The line went dead.

"That's odd," Harrison said out loud and pressed the end button on his cell phone just to be sure it disconnected.

"What's odd?" Douglas asked.

"That was the gas attendant from yesterday. What was his name again?"

"Bubba Hanks," Douglas answered.

"Yeah, that guy."

"They do own a tow truck," Barbara said. "Last night I saw it when we responded to that accident."

"I think they have it," Harrison said.

"Did Bubba say he did?" Douglas asked.

"No. In fact, he said he didn't have it. But I'm sure he was lying. Where do they take the cars they tow?"

Douglas and Barbara exchanged looks and shrugs.

"Don't know," Barbara answered.

"But I know where the family lives," Douglas said. "We could always drive by and check it out."

"Sure," Harrison answered.

Douglas stood up and Harrison followed.

"I'll keep calling just in case," Barbara said while the two men headed for the door. "Don't forget we're having dinner out tonight."

Back in the truck, Harrison sat in the passenger seat watching the road ahead anxiously. Adrenaline coursed through his body in waves switching between anger and apprehension.

Douglas turned left once they crossed the bridge and headed east following the south bank of the Rogue River. The road wound around the hillside with trees blocking the view of the river at times. They rounded one more turn and the view opened up. A sign in front of a long house read, Indian Creek Café. Several cars were parked in front. Douglas drove on by and turned off onto a narrow gravel road that passed between two hills.

A dust cloud bellowed up behind the truck while Douglas continued at a faster speed than Harrison felt comfortable. He could have sworn he felt the truck sliding on the gravel so he gripped the handle above the door and held on.

Suddenly Douglas slammed on the brakes. The truck fishtailed but Douglas kept it under control and brought it to a stop. Stopped in the middle of the road beneath an arch that reminded Harrison of the one Douglas and Barbara had at the end of their drive was a police SUV. A short, stocky man in a policeman's uniform stood in front of the car with his stubby arms folded over his chest. He grimaced and turned his face away as the dust cloud caught up and passed in front of the truck. Once it dissipated, the officer approached Douglas's window.

"Damn it, Doug," the officer greeted and coughed. "Where the hell do you think you're goin' in such a hurry? The speed is fifteen on this road."

"Sorry, Judd," Douglas apologized but Harrison didn't hear any tone of sincerity.

"What're you doin' out here?" Judd asked.

"Got a call you're having some issues with your phone?" Douglas lied.

"No," Judd shook his head. "Phone's fine. Who ya got with ya?" Judd raised his head and craned his neck to get a better look at Harrison.

"Oh, this is my old friend from Portland, Harrison. He's just down for a visit." Another lie, or maybe a half-lie, Harrison noted.

"Well, ya might as well turn around here. We aint havin' any trouble. Besides, this here is private property, ya need to call before ya drop by, otherwise you're trespassing' and we don't take kindly to trespassers." Judd pointed to the sign hung on the gatepost.

"If you're sure," Douglas said. "But since I'm already here I could check it out just to be safe. It's no trouble, really."

"I told ya' we aint havin' any trouble. Now move along before I give you a ticket for disturbing the peace."

"Okay, have a good one," Douglas said and threw the truck in reverse.

Harrison kept his eye on the officer who appeared to be doing the same to him.

Once the truck was turned around and they were headed back to the main road, Harrison spoke up. "That was the Police Chief, wasn't it?" The one you said was related to the guy at the gas station."

"Yes, he's the one I was telling you about."

"Did you notice he seemed to be waiting for us? I mean, his car wasn't even running. How would he know we'd be coming?"

"I suspect Bubba called to warn him. I don't know." Douglas answered. "Something isn't adding up. I mean, your car missing, finding all of those license plates, the way Judd wouldn't let us onto his property...they're up to something."

The rest of the trip back to the house was quiet. Harrison kept thinking about what Douglas had said and about finding Thomas' plate among those they found. *Douglas was right; something was going on in this town.*

Once back at the house, Barbara informed them that she'd had no luck with the rest of the towing companies. In fact, they all said they hadn't received a call for a tow from the County in months. Douglas filled her in on their run in with Judd and she agreed it sounded suspicious.

"Well, you two should get cleaned up and changed so we can go to dinner," she ended the conversation.

Back in the bedroom, Harrison looked through his suitcase. He pulled out a neatly folded Hawaiian shirt and a pair of brown Dockers. Just when he kicked off his shoes, his cell phone rang. He looked at the display and answered.

"Hi, Justus."

"You were supposed to call me last night," Justus said, sounding a little hurt.

"Sorry, it slipped my mind."

"Well I've been worried. What's going on?"

Harrison sat down on the edge of the bed and filled Justus in on the last two days. Justus quietly listened and when Harrison was finished, the line was silent for what seemed like a long time.

"You still there?" Harrison asked.

"Yes. I'm just in shock. How are you going to find Thomas—or, or, get home?"

"I don't know. I'm going to try to file another report with the county tomorrow and then notify my insurance company. I have rental coverage; perhaps it will help in this case?"

"I hope so," Justus said.

"So, how was work?" Harrison hated to bring it up.

"Not the same without you there."

"You'll survive," Harrison said and shook his head. He could hear the sad puppy-dog expression in Justus' tone.

"Debra is still up to her tricks. She managed to get Jackie canned."

"Jackie? What did she do?"

"She allegedly misfiled several papers and was late punching in three days in a row. She swears she was on time and that she never even touched the papers but Eric still fired her. I heard the union is getting involved."

"Good," Harrison said. He wished he had the union to fall back on but being low management, he didn't have that luxury. "Well, I have to be going."

"Going? Where?" Justus asked. Again the feeling that he was missing out on fun registered in his tone.

"Dinner. Doug's wife Barbara wants to go out tonight." Harrison answered. "It's nothing great. Believe me, it's just dinner."

"Okay. Call me tomorrow night?"

"Sure." Harrison touched the red disconnect dot on his phone's screen and continued changing his clothes.

CHAPTER SEVEN

Harrison lay in bed staring at the ceiling. He had been awake for the better part of an hour. Everything was so quiet that even the slightest creak in the floor or chirp from a robin outside sounded like thunder. It was quite different than back home in Portland. He had become used to sleeping through the noises of the night: traffic on the street, the occasional siren, dogs barking and the neighbors loud arguments.

When he heard stirrings in the kitchen, he threw back the covers and started his day.

Barbara was up and had just started a fresh pot of coffee. She was dressed in her EMT uniform.

"You're up early," Harrison greeted her.

She looked at him and smiled. "I start my regular shift, twenty-four on, forty-eight off."

"That's what you work?" Harrison was shocked.

"Yes, just like the firemen. We work a twenty-four hour shift and then have two days off. It averages itself out by the end of the month."

"Good grief, I would die if I had to work like that."

Barbara laughed. "We aren't working the entire time. We have a lot of down time. But it did take a bit of getting used to."

When the coffee was finished, she filled her thermos before turning back to Harrison. "Want a cup? There's still a little left."

"You should have it."

"I'll make another for you and Doug."

Harrison sat down at the table and checked his phone for any texts. None. Once Barbara started the next pot, she joined him.

"So, what's on the plan for today?" she asked and took a sip of her coffee.

"First I'm going to stop by the Sheriff's office and fill out a report. Then I'll call my insurance company. See if I can get a rental car."

"That might be hard. The nearest car rental place is in Crescent City or you could go north to Coos Bay."

"Oh," Harrison sighed. "I don't suppose they deliver?"

"Not out here." Barbara shook her head. "I'm sure Doug would drive you, though."

"I would hate to impose. You both have been so gracious already letting me stay here."

"It's no problem." Barbara smiled. "What about finding your friend? Any ideas on that?"

"Once I get this car thing figured out, I'll start checking the motels in town."

"You'll find them all at the south end around the fair grounds. That should make it easier."

"Good."

"Well, I've got to run." Barbara gulped down the last of her coffee and put her cup in the sink. "See you tomorrow," she said and grabbed her thermos.

"Okay. Have a good day." Harrison called as she closed the front door behind her. He looked at the coffeemaker on the kitchen counter. It was ready. He poured himself a cup and started back to the table but stopped when he nearly bumped into Douglas.

Douglas, dressed in his plaid boxer shorts and nothing else, jumped.

"Oh, you're up," he gasped, not completely awake himself. "Sorry."

"No worries," Harrison assured him. "It's your house."

"Barbara gone?"

"Yes, she just left."

"Ah, coffee." Douglas took a mug from the cupboard and poured himself a cup. He joined Harrison at the table. "I have a couple appointments this morning."

"That's okay. Could you drop me off at the courthouse? I want to file a report and then contact my insurance company about a possible car rental."

"Sure." Douglas agreed and nodded. "I should be finished about one or two."

"That would work. I can check out some of the motels in town then."

An hour later, Douglas pulled the truck over to the curb across from the courthouse. "I'll meet you for a late lunch at the Port Hole."

"Sounds good. Thanks for the lift." Harrison said. He stepped back on the sidewalk and watched the truck drive off.

He took a deep breath when he looked at the courthouse building. Remembering the deputy from the day before made him feel nervous. Once the traffic cleared, he hurried across the street and up the front walk.

It didn't take long to make it through security. The older deputy pointed out the sheriff's office even though Harrison didn't need directions. His anxiety grew with each step. The thought of having to deal with the same insensitive deputy from the day before caused his pulse to quicken and his hands to tremble. Opening the door, Harrison felt his body relax. Behind the counter was a younger man with a pleasant smile.

"'Morning," he greeted Harrison.

"Good morning," Harrison returned while he approached the counter. "I need to report a stolen car. I called all the companies on this list," he handed it to the deputy, "and they all said they didn't tow any cars two nights ago."

"I see," the deputy said looking at the list with a puzzled expression. "Uh, who gave you this?"

"The deputy who was here yesterday. Why, is something wrong?"

"Oh, good grief, I'm sorry about that. This is the list we use to investigate missing cars. Just a moment and I'll get your information."

Twenty minutes later Harrison walked out of the courthouse with a copy of his incident report in his hand. He looked at his watch and decided to head toward the opposite end of town where Barbara said the motels were. While walking, he phoned his insurance agent only to get a recording that her office was closed for an extended weekend, something about a wedding. Harrison didn't listen to it all. He just hung up and kept walking.

About two blocks from the courthouse, Harrison noticed a sign, "Wild Rivers Inn." He looked down the side street and glimpsed the end of a motel building tucked behind a hardware store. From the little bit he could see, the building appeared in need of a good painting and had no view. *No, Thomas wouldn't have stayed there.* He decided to skip it.

Continuing south, he passed the blue police station on his right and then a Dairy Queen to his left. He thought about stopping to get a light snack but noticed they weren't open for another ninety minutes. Just past the Subway Sandwich Shop, Harrison spotted another motel sign, "Rhododendron Lodge." The single story motel sat parallel to the highway and didn't appear to be that uninviting except for the weathered, paint chipped, sign. *Thomas might have stayed here.* While he walked up the small rise to the office, Harrison wondered why the motel was named Rhododendron when there wasn't a bush in sight.

The unmistakable, pungent odor of patchouli oil stuck him the moment he opened the front door. He hesitated a second to take in a deep breath of the outside air before entering. The motel office was nothing special. A room about the size of his living room back home was all there was to the lobby. A counter divided the room in half which made the space feel that much smaller. Harrison approached the counter and rang the small bell. Instantly a woman with long, frizzy blonde hair, dressed like a left-over hippy from the early 1970's came out of the back room. She smiled at Harrison then pulled out a large black binder from beneath the counter.

"Looking for a room?" she said in a gravelly smoker's voice.

Harrison smiled. "No, I'm actually looking for a friend of mine."

"Oh no," the woman shook her head and closed the binder. "I can't give you any information about a guest. We have rules here."

"No, no. I just want to know if you've seen him or his car. He went missing about a week ago." Harrison took

Thomas' picture from his pocket and held it up for the woman to see. She hesitated at first and then took a look.

"Nice looking fella. He your boyfriend?"

"No. Just a friend," Harrison answered, trying not to sound annoyed by her comment.

"You a cop?"

"No."

"One of them private dicks?"

It took Harrison a second to understand she meant a private investigator. "No," he answered.

"Nope, I aint seen him," she said and shook her head. The edges of her mouth were turned down in a prissy, couldn't-care-less sort of frown. Then she looked at the photo of the Cadillac and her expression changed. "However, I have seen this caddy."

"You have?" Harrison gasped.

"Yeah, it was, oh…" she looked up toward the ceiling. "When did you say your friend went missin'?"

"A week ago last Tuesday."

"Nah, it wasn't his. I seen this just yesterday."

"Where?"

"Driving around town. Ol' Judd Hanks owns it. Hear he bought it out of the abandoned lot."

A chill ran through Harrison's body. "Are you sure?"

"Yeah, I'm sure. My youngest boy works for him and that's what he told me. My boy don't lie."

"Thanks," Harrison said. He looked at the photo for a second and then tucked it back into his pocket.

"Now, don't be goin' and telling anyone I said that, 'cause if anyone asks, I'll deny it. We got a reputation here of keeping our mouths shut, ya see. Our guests want to know they can trust us to keep their secrets."

"I won't." Harrison assured her and left. Just being in the office, Harrison felt as though he needed a shower. That alone convinced more than ever that Thomas would not have patronized this motel. Thomas was too fastidious to stay in such a place. *I'm sure they have roaches or bed bugs or worse.*

Across from the county fairground's entrance Harrison came to another motel. This motel was a large, yellow, two-story building built at the edge of the sidewalk. The sign above the drive through portico read, Pacific View Inn. Harrison turned around to see the view. Rather than there being a wide, panoramic view, Harrison caught just a peek at the ocean between the fairgrounds building and another building nearby. He shook his head and went inside.

A few minutes later he came out. It had been a total waste of time. The woman behind the counter wouldn't even look at the photo and insisted she knew nothing about any missing tourist or a Cadillac. Harrison knew she was lying because he hadn't mentioned the make of the car or pulled that photo out of his pocket. He looked around while he stood on the corner. For the first time he noticed that Highway 101, which ran through the middle of town, was renamed Ellensburg Avenue. He waited until there was no traffic and then ran across the four lane highway.

Directly behind a small stone building with the sign Chowder Bowl Restaurant was another motel. This one actually had ocean views. The sign by the highway read, Sea Drifter. Harrison looked back across the street at the Pacific View and thought it was too bad the names weren't switched.

The young, front desk clerk at the Sea Drifter was pleasant enough but he hadn't seen anyone resembling Thomas or the car. Harrison thanked him and headed back to the street.

The Pacific side of the highway, unlike the inland side,

had no defined sidewalk, but Harrison only had one more motel to check and it was right next door.

Walking into the lobby of the Ocean Front Inn, Harrison was sure Thomas would have made the Inn his first choice. The lobby was much grander than the others in town. It had a large seating area with a sofa and two big, plush chairs. A coffee table sat in the middle of the arrangement. A stone fireplace with seashells set in the mortar made the lounge area more inviting. Just beyond the lounge were a gift shop and a coffee shop. Harrison noticed a hallway branching off toward the west and assumed it led to the guest rooms. While he waited for the clerk to finish with her two guests, he looked at the front desk, a long counter topped with shiny grey granite mixed with bits of silver. On the front of the counter was a wood carving of an ocean scene.

The clerk, a pleasant appearing young woman in a neatly pressed white blouse and maroon vest, looked at him and smiled. "I'll be right with you."

Harrison nodded and waited until the two women gathered their suitcases and headed for the door.

"How may I help you?" she asked.

Just then a maid wheeled her cart into the lobby. The clerk behind the counter leaned forward and gave a disapproving look.

"I'm sorry," the short, young woman dressed in a maroon shirt dress and white apron apologized. "The guest in 202 left these behind."

The clerk snatched the two articles of clothing out of the maid's hands and quickly stashed them under the counter, out of sight.

"Rosa, how many times do I have to tell you not to interrupt a guest or bring your cart into the lobby?" the clerk snapped.

"I'm sorry, Miss Hanks," the young maid apologized in her thick Spanish accent. She ducked her head and slowly crept back to her cart.

"I apologize for that," Miss Hanks said and smiled at Harrison. "You were saying?"

Harrison smiled though he wanted to reprimand the clerk for the unprofessional and outright mean way she handled her employee but he shrugged it off.

"I'm looking for a friend of mine and wondered if by chance he had stayed here a week ago last Tuesday. He's about my height, thin, dark brown hair, neatly trimmed beard. I have his picture here," he pulled out the photograph of Thomas and held it up.

"Nope. No one like that stayed here," she said without looking at the photograph.

"He was driving a white pearl, Cadillac Deville," Harrison continued.

"No. I haven't seen either one." Miss Hanks said shaking her head. "Do you want a room?"

"No." Harrison answered.

"Then I must ask you to leave." Miss Hanks' friendly tone turned ice cold.

Harrison took a step back and glanced at the maid who was just out of sight of the clerk. The expression on Rosa's face gave him the feeling she wanted to tell him something. He looked back at the clerk.

"I'll be having lunch at the Port Hole if you think of anything. My name is Harrison Andrews and my cell number is…" he gave his phone number slowly just in case the maid was able to write it down.

"Yeah, yeah, I won't need it," Miss Hanks said. "Now

are you going to leave?"

"Yes. Thank you for your time and hospitality." Without glancing at the maid, Harrison left and returned to the street. He looked at his watch and noticed it was nearing one. He had a mile and a half walk to the Port Hole ahead of him. Looking at his phone, he started walking.

About a third of the way, he passed in front of the police station. The parking lot was empty. He glanced at his watch and decided to take a little detour. He quickened his pace and headed down the side street to see if there was an employee parking lot in back and if the Cadillac was there. In just a few moments his questions were answered. There was a parking lot and to his surprise, the white pearl, Deville was tucked neatly away from the others near the back entrance to the building. With his pulse racing, he turned around and hurried back to the main road and toward the north end of town.

The sun was hot but there was a cool breeze blowing down at the docks. Harrison wiped his brow with the back of his hand and looked at the carved wood sign that hung from a bar above the door. Port Hole Pub and Eatery it read in an Old English font. Harrison guessed it was made to resemble the old pubs in the pirate movie *Treasure Island*. Even the building itself was rustic and played the part.

Harrison opened the door and walked inside. The interior continued the pirate theme. A beautifully carved masthead of a fair maiden bursting out of her bodice adorned the front of the hostess' station and greeted customers. Tables were arranged along the outer walls on both sides of the door. A few were scattered in the center of the room. A lunch counter that also served as the bar stretched across the back of the Pub. At the end of the bar stood a cluster of tall pub tables and stools.

Two old men he suspected were fishermen based on their tanned and weathered faces and their thick, rough, work worn hands were seated at the counter. They turned and looked over their shoulders at Harrison. They both gave him the once over and then began to whisper to each other while they turned back around. A couple seated at a table in the middle of the room looked at him for a second and then resumed their conversation. The hostess, dressed as a barmaid, hurried over to greet him.

"Ahoy, sailor," she smiled at him.

Harrison smiled. Nothing about the woman's perfectly styled hair, pulled back in a cascade of auburn curls, and make-up screamed wench. "Ahoy," Harrison answered playing along.

"Will you be dining alone?"

"No, there will be two of us. My friend must be running a bit late."

"Sure," she said and nodded. Her ruby lips curled in an attractive smile. She plucked two menus from behind the masthead. "Right this way."

"I'm sorry, but could I have that table in the corner?" Harrison asked and pointed to a table in the opposite direction from the rest of the diners.

The hostess looked puzzled and her smile slipped but she regained herself. "Sure." She led the way over to the table. "Would you care for a pint while you wait?"

Harrison frowned and shuddered. "Could I get rum and coke instead?" he answered and gave her a smile.

"Be right back." She gave a slight curtsy before hurrying away.

The front door opened and a small bell tinkled. Harrison looked up from reading the menu hoping to see Douglas but instead closed and lowered it. He stood up in order to catch the eye of the motel maid.

Rosa stood by the hostess station and looked around the pub. When she spotted Harrison, she hurried over to him.

"Hola," she said quietly.

"Please, have a seat," Harrison said and motioned toward the chair across from him.

Rosa appeared to be nervous. Several times she looked over her shoulder at the men at the bar or the couple across the room.

Harrison pulled Thomas' photo from his pocket and slid it across the table.

"Have you seen this man?"

"Sí, señor Tomas," she answered and nodded.

"Was he staying at your motel?"

"Sí, but he disappear."

"What do you mean?"

"He check in and Miss Hanks ask me to show him to room 220, at the end of the hall. So, I take him to his room. He give me ten dollars and tell me to keep it.

"The next morning, Miss Hanks tells me to clean up room 220 and pack up señor Tomas' things into his suitcase. She tell me he not come back. He decide to leave in hurry."

Harrison sat back in stunned silence.

"I go to his room. It was a mess. Like someone had a fight in there. I pick up señor Tomas' things and put them in his suitcase. I take it to Miss Hanks and she throws it into the incinerator."

"What?" Harrison gasped.

"But I not give her his wallet," Rosa continued. She cautiously slid it across the table. "I have his laptop computer back at mi casa. I give it to you."

"Where?"

She took a paper napkin and with a pen from the hotel, wrote down her address and again carefully slid it across the table.

"You come tonight. I take mi hijo to his abuela. I be home by six." She stood up.

"Ok. I will come."

She nodded and then quietly slipped out the door and was gone.

"Your guest left already?" the waitress, a young woman dressed in the same costume as the hostess, asked when she set Harrison's rum and coke down.

"Uh, yeah, but she wasn't—"

Harrison stopped when he realized she wasn't listening. She was already halfway back to the kitchen. He looked around the bar. The two sailors were gone. The pub seemed deserted except for him. Not even the hostess was in sight. Harrison sipped his drink and stared at the address on the napkin.

The minutes seemed to pass like hours. Harrison looked at his watch. Douglas was late. Lunch was rapidly turning into an early dinner. The waitress came over to check on him.

"Would you like to order?" she asked.

"Uh, sure," he answered. "I'll have the fish and chips."

"Another rum and coke?"

"Sure."

He watched her walk back behind the bar and give the order through a small pass-through window to the kitchen. Music played quietly from the ceiling speakers.

Just when his fish and chips were delivered, the pub door opened. Douglas had arrived. Harrison smiled and waved him over.

"Sorry, I'm late," he apologized. "I'll have what he's having," he told the waitress.

"A rum and coke, also?"

Douglas grimaced. "Is that what you're drinking?" He looked at Harrison. "No, a pint for me," he answered, sitting down across from Harrison. The waitress hurried away.

"Busy day?"

"I'll say. A line was pulled down by the tree pruners working south of town. As soon as I fixed that, another line came down north of town near the road construction. If I didn't know better, I'd say they were done on purpose."

Harrison felt a chill.

"How was your morning?" Douglas asked.

"Busy. I filed the report on my car. Then I hit the motels. I found out Thomas checked into the Ocean Front. Hey, is everyone in this town named Hanks?"

Douglas laughed. "Why?"

"The desk clerk at the Ocean Front was a Miss Hanks."

"Oh yes, Melody Hanks. She's one of Judd's daughters. Why?"

"She denied recognizing Thomas but the maid, Rosa, she said that this Hanks woman checked him in. Then the next day, she told Rosa to clean out his room and bring his things to her."

"What did she want with his things?"

"She burned them. All except for this." Harrison showed Douglas the wallet. "And his laptop. Rosa has it and said if I come by her place after six, she would give it to me."

"Great! We can swing by after we finish here. But what happened to your friend?"

"She doesn't know. He just disappeared. She did say the room was thrashed. So, whatever happened, he didn't go

94

willingly."

"That's odd," Douglas said. He looked away while he appeared to think.

"Here you go," the waitress interrupted and set a basket of fish and chips and a pint down on the table in front of Douglas. "Will there be anything else?" she asked.

Harrison noticed she was looking at Thomas' wallet still lying on the table. He discreetly took it and put it back into his pocket.

"No. I think we're fine," Douglas answered.

The waitress forced a smile and left.

"She's different," Harrison whispered.

Douglas laughed quietly. "She's another one of Judd's kids. Serena Hanks."

"How many kids does this guy have?" Harrison asked and looked across the room where the hostess was talking on her phone.

"I think ten, but don't quote me on that."

"I think we should hurry up and get out of here," Harrison said. An uneasy feeling began to come over him.

"Sure," Douglas agreed and called the hostess back over. He requested a to-go box and transferred his meal to the Styrofoam container. He gulped down his beer and left the bill and tip on the table. "Thanks, Serena," he called as the two left.

Harrison jumped into the passenger seat of Douglas's truck. Douglas took his place behind the wheel and started up the engine. Glancing over his shoulder, Harrison saw a police cruiser turning into the parking lot. Douglas put the truck in gear and started out. The cruiser pulled into a spot right in front of the pub. He didn't follow them and Harrison relaxed.

Just when they pulled onto the main road through town,

a siren blared behind them. Harrison jumped. Douglas pulled the truck over to the side of the road and stopped. The cruiser sped past them. Harrison gave an audible sigh of relief.

"For a moment I thought he was after us," he admitted to Douglas.

"For what?"

"I don't know. I guess I'm just a little paranoid after talking with the maid and seeing how the people in the restaurant stared."

"Well, let's just swing by her place and see if we can get the laptop."

Douglas turned right when they reached Fifth Street. He followed the narrow road down a small hill to where it turned right into a mobile home park. Douglas hit the brakes. Right in front of them, about the middle of the block, were two police cruisers, a rescue ambulance and a fire truck, all with lights flashing. A small group of curious neighbors gathered across from what Harrison assumed was the house with the emergency.

A policeman standing behind his cruiser on the side of the street waved Douglas through. Slowly Douglas obeyed. While the truck crept along the wrong side of the street, Harrison looked at the house numbers.

"Douglas!" he nearly shouted.

Douglas hit the brakes and the truck lurched forward as it stopped.

"What?"

"It's the house." Harrison said looking at the napkin and again at the number on the end of the blue mobile home.

"There's Barbara," Douglas said and waved his wife over.

Barbara rushed over to Harrison's window.

"What are you two doing here?" she asked.

"Harrison was supposed to meet someone named Rosa here."

Barbara looked at Harrison.

"She was going to give me Thomas' laptop."

"You best go. I'll see what I can do," she said.

"What's going on?" Douglas asked.

"I can't get into it now. You should go."

"Okay. See you in the morning," Douglas said and slowly started up.

Harrison watched in the side mirror. Barbara headed back into the house.

"What do you suppose happened?"

"I have no idea, but I'm sure we'll find out in the morning."

Back at the house, Harrison called Danika and filled her in on what had transpired.

"I can't believe someone stole your car," she said.

"Who stole a car?" Harrison heard Robert's voice in the background.

"Harry's. Someone stole Harry's Bug," she answered.

"Did he report it to the police?"

"Yes, but they won't do anything."

"Let me see what I can do. I met a few guys from Oregon at a Law Enforcement Seminar last fall. Maybe they can do something."

"That would be great," Danika said and returned to her conversation with Harrison.

"Aside from all the weird stuff going on here, I think you would really like Ellensburg. It reminds me of how dad used to talk about what Hillsboro was like when he was a kid."

"I don't know, Harry. It might be too small and

backward."

"True," Harrison agreed. "Once I find Thomas, I'm heading back to Portland as fast as I can."

Danika laughed. They ended their conversation with their usual I love you's.

Harrison looked at his watch. It was late but he had promised to check in with Justus. He dialed Justus' cell number and sat back against the headboard on the bed.

"Hi!" Justus answered in a cheerful tone that sounded too wide awake for the late hour.

"Is that music I hear?"

"Uh, yes," Justus answered.

Harrison could tell that Justus covered the mouthpiece on his phone. When he came back, the music was still playing but a lot quieter.

"You best not be having a party."

"I'm not, honest."

"Justus, I told you the rules—"

"I know, I'm not having a party, I swear. I'm just listening to music."

"Well, keep it down. It's late and I don't need the neighbors calling the police."

"Ok," Justus answered in a submissive tone. "So, what's up?"

Harrison ran through the events of the day and after a few questions about work the conversation went quiet.

"I guess I'll let you go—"

"Oh, wait! I almost forgot," Justus interrupted.

"What?"

"Don't be surprised if you get a call from Eric. There's been a lot of sh—stuff coming down at work about your being gone. Several of your clients aren't happy about it and they've gone over Eric's head. So, don't be surprised if you get a call from *the boss*."

"Interesting."

"Yeah, one of the big wigs from the head office in Denver even flew into town today to have a meeting with him. I just happened to be outside his office and heard some raised voices."

"Well, I'm sure it's nothing."

"That's not what I heard. I think Eric may be in a bit of hot water himself."

"Thanks for keeping an ear open. I've really got to get some sleep," Harrison said.

"Okay, night."

"Thanks again, Justus." Harrison repeated.

Justus disconnected the call before Harrison had a chance to press the end button on his smart phone display. Setting his cell phone on the nightstand beside the bed, Harrison slid down and was fast asleep.

CHAPTER EIGHT

Harrison awoke to the sound of talking in another room. He rolled onto his back and looked at the window. Sunlight seeped into the bedroom around the edges of the window shade. He looked at his watch. It was already after nine. He threw the blankets aside and quickly dressed. After making the bed, he went to find out what happened to Rosa.

Barbara and Douglas were at the table. The coffee pot sat in the center with an empty cup.

"Someone was tired," Douglas teased when he saw Harrison.

"I guess all that walking yesterday wore me out." He took the coffee pot and poured himself a cup. Slipping into the chair across from Barbara, he took a sip from his cup and looked at his hosts.

The expression on Barbara's face seemed serious.

"What happened?" he asked.

"Harrison, Rosa is dead." Douglas answered.

"What?" Harrison nearly shouted and lunged forward in his chair. "How?"

"I don't know for sure. When I arrived on the scene, the police were already there. An officer showed me to the bathroom where I found her. She was lying on the bathroom floor. She had been stabbed several times and blood was everywhere. It was obvious she was gone and that she put up a real fight," Barbara explained.

"That doesn't make any sense. Who would do such a thing to her?" Harrison was in shock. His ears heard what Barbara had said but his mind was having a hard time processing the words.

"I heard Chief Hanks talking to the coroner outside when I was leaving. He was telling him it appeared to be a classic case of a homeowner stumbling in on a burglar."

"A burglar? What?" Harrison repeated sounding confused.

"That's what he said," Barbara shook her head and looked at her coffee. "But I'm not buying it. Normally someone who breaks into a home goes for the nearest exit when he hears someone coming. He doesn't kick in the bathroom door to get at the hiding homeowner much less slam her head against the toilet and stab her repeatedly. I don't understand why he ignored all of that evidence."

"Did you say anything to the him?" Douglas asked.

"And risk losing my job?" Barbara shook her head. "One thing I've learned, you don't question the Chief or contradict him, especially in front of another high ranking official.

"This seems too coincidental. I mean, this happens right after she tells me about Thomas and gives me his wallet."

"True. It's obvious she was trying to get away from whoever it was and locked herself in the bathroom. Maybe after the coroner examines her body he will clear things up." Douglas added.

"What about the laptop?" Harrison asked. "She said she had it and was going to give it to me."

"I don't know if this is it," Barbara answered. She picked the laptop case up from beside her chair and set it on the table.

"It is!" Harrison gasped and grabbed it. "Where did you find it?"

"When I arrived, I noticed the police were in the back bedrooms tearing them apart. So, I figured they were looking for something specific and I figured it was the laptop. I didn't hold out much hope of being able to find it. Then I thought about if it were me where would I hide something. So, while I was leaving, I pretended I was a bit sick and needed a glass of water. I went into the kitchen and looked behind the refrigerator. No one ever pulls those things out, not even to clean behind them. That's where I found it."

"Didn't anyone notice?"

"No. They were still in the back. I just put the strap over my shoulder and tucked it between my body and the medical equipment. Then I just walked back to the truck. No one even gave me a second look."

"That's genius!" Douglas praised his wife.

"I'll say." Harrison answered.

"Why's it so important?" Barbara asked.

"Thomas keeps his journal on it. Every night before he goes to bed, he religiously writes about his day. So, I'm hoping he wrote something before he disappeared that will give us an idea of what happened and what's going on."

"Well, open it up and let's find out," Douglas prodded.

Harrison unzipped the black cloth case and reached

inside. He pulled out the laptop and opened it. The monitor screen was cracked. He felt the hope inside him dim. He pressed the power button. Nothing happened. He reached into the bag again and pulled out the power cord. After plugging it in, he pressed the power button again. This time he heard the fan inside start up. Moments later an image appeared on the broken monitor.

"We're in business!" he announced. He glanced up at Barbara and Douglas. Everyone was smiling with renewed hope.

Once the start-up was complete, he accessed Thomas' journal. Thomas had begun each new day at the top of the Journal, pushing the day before down, into the past. Harrison's hands began to tremble from nervousness and excitement.

"He wrote something," he said then cleared his throat.

"Today I started my annual trip to visit mom and dad in San Diego. Harrison fixed me a nice going away breakfast but he knows I can't eat before a long trip. Still I managed to eat a little so as not to hurt his feelings.

I hit rain around Salem. Traffic slowed but not too bad. I was still able to make good time. I did see one accident though, well, the aftermath actually. It looked like a little Mazda3 hit a Ford F150. Not pretty. There was a sheet covering what I assumed was a body on the side of the highway. People need to slow down and be more careful in this weather!

I stopped for a quick pit break at the McDonald's in Creswell. The next chance to stop is on the coast. I did grab a Coke and a couple double cheeseburgers to-go since I'll hit lunch between Drain and Reedsport.

I stopped to get gas at a little mom and pop gas station

in Port Orford. The attendant there reminded me of that creepy gas attendant in the movie, Urban Legend. I didn't get a look at his name but the place was called Hanks. I think he did something to my car. It started acting funny the minute I left the station. I made it as far as the viewpoint just north of town before I had to pull over. I hitched a ride into town with a nice lady on her way to Brookings. In the short time with her she told me she was recently widowed and was on her way back home after a memorial up north. Harrison would have been in tears had he been here. He takes empathy to the extreme.

Every one of the garages in this Podunk town was closed and the place where I actually found someone, the owner refused to open up. He said I'll have to wait until morning.

I checked into the Ocean Front Inn not too far from the towing company. I wanted to be close so I could get them first thing in the morning.

The clerk at the motel here was very nice. She gave me a room away from the other guests and a complimentary bottle of wine. She also had a nice little Spanish maid show me to my room. After unlocking the door for me, the maid said something odd. She told me not to drink the wine. I wasn't planning on it anyway. I don't like the stuff. I'll save it for Harrison. He drinks it like water. That's all for today.

It's now eleven o'clock. I guess the motel is filled because there are noisy people next door. I didn't realize this room had an adjoining door. I should have asked for a different room. I'm not going to get any sleep tonight."

Harrison sat and stared at the cracked screen. After a few moments he looked up at Barbara and Douglas. Both sat with stunned expressions.

"I knew it!" Harrison snapped. "I knew something was wrong when we found Thomas' license plate discarded up there."

"What's going on?" Douglas asked sounding more pensive. "I mean, it's too much of a coincidence for both your cars to have died at the same spot. And what is going on at that motel?"

"This is getting serious," Barbara added. "I'm going to talk to the pathologist who assists the coroner and see if she'll tell me what happened to Rosa."

"Be careful," Harrison warned. "If they killed her over this laptop then there is no telling what they might do."

"Believe me, I will be," Barbara assured him.

While Barbara slept and Douglas was called away on a job, Harrison took a stroll around the yard. He couldn't stop thinking about everything he'd learned: that Thomas's car had broken down at the same place his Bug had, that Thomas had stayed at the Ocean Front Inn but why didn't they charge his credit card? Another concern to him was Thomas' car being driven by the chief of police.

Several times he pulled out his cell phone and started to call Danika but stopped. It was Saturday and that was the day she spent with the boys. Unfortunately it was also Robert's day off, which meant he was usually home. Danika had warned Harrison that Robert didn't like her talking to him during family time. However, Harrison knew it didn't matter which day he called, Robert didn't like him talking to Danika at all.

Harrison hadn't realized it but he had made his way to the large arch over the driveway that marked the boundary of the Blair's property. He looked up at the top beam and wondered how they managed to hoist it up so high. It was nearly twenty feet to the top of the posts. He stood staring at the beam and then an uneasy feeling crept up on him. He turned and looked around. There was no one in sight except for a parked car at the end of the neighbor's driveway across the street. Harrison turned around and headed back to the house.

Shortly after three, Douglas pulled into the driveway. From the living room window, Harrison watched him park his work truck beside Barbara's Honda SUV. Thoughts of his own car came to mind. He wished he had it. Then he wouldn't feel so helpless. He should be out there searching for Thomas instead of being housebound. He turned around when Douglas walked into the house.

"How'd it go?" he asked.

"Fine," Douglas answered and hung his coat on the handrail at the foot of the stairs. "I heard some strange news from old lady Somers, though."

"Who's she?" Harrison asked and followed Douglas into the kitchen.

"She's one of the town's oldest residents and quite the busy-body. If you ever want to know what's happening around here, just ask her." Douglas took a bottle of beer from the refrigerator and offered one to Harrison before shutting the door and continuing. "She said she was at the police station yesterday and a couple came in to report their son went missing over a month ago. Seems he was driving alone up the coast to meet some friends in Newport but never made it. They showed Chief Hanks a copy of a bank statement that showed their son had stayed at the Ocean Front Inn."

Harrison shuddered visibly and suddenly his legs felt week. He grabbed the back of a chair at the table, pulled it out and sat down.

"What did he say?" Harrison asked.

"Nothing much. Ms. Somers said he acted very professional even though the mother was sobbing and quite upset. He just took the report and told them he'd look into it. It wasn't until they left that it got interesting."

"Why's that?"

"Because he tossed the report in the trash," Douglas answered and took a long drink of his beer.

"He did that in front of the Somers woman?" Harrison was beginning to doubt the story.

"Yeah, and when she called him on it, she said he made up an excuse about being short staffed and not having time to look into every missing person report that comes in. Besides, he told her, there isn't any proof any of them are still around."

"Any of them?" Harrison repeated thinking Douglas made a mistake.

"That's right, *them*," Douglas repeated. "There are more. Evidently, Ms. Somers talked to Janie, the receptionist at the station and found that in the last three months, five other men have gone missing, and Chief Hanks hasn't done a thing about it. What did he say when you filed a missing person report on your friend?"

"I haven't filed one with him," Harrison admitted.

"Then that's our next step. We know that he stayed at Ocean Front and that his car broke down at the viewpoint. That pins him to Ellensburg." Douglas took another drink.

"Okay. I guess we have a plan."

That evening Harrison phoned Justus. Again when Justus answered, loud music was blaring in the background.

"Justus, what is going on there?" he demanded.

"Nothing."

"Who's there? I heard laughing."

"No one."

Harrison could tell by the way Justus stammered and the sound became muffled that Justus was lying. When Justus uncovered his phone, the music and talking were gone. Harrison figured Justus had gone outside.

"You better not be having a party—"

"Why would you think such a terrible thing? I know the rules," Justus interrupted sounding hurt but Harrison knew it was a ruse.

"The neighbors will let me know. Anyway, I have something really important for you to do."

"Shoot!"

"I need you to go into Thomas' bedroom and in the top drawer of his dresser you'll find the title to his car. I need the VIN off it."

"VIN?" Justus questioned.

"It's the long number mixed with letters. Get the title and I can tell you where to look."

"Okay."

"One other thing," Harrison warned. "No snooping around in his room. Just get the title and then get out."

"Got it."

A few moments later, Harrison ended the call. He sat on the bed in the guest room and looked at the number he had written down. Thoughts of what he would say in the morning flooded his mind and caused his stomach to tighten with nervousness.

CHAPTER NINE

A thick fog covered the coastline when Harrison finally rolled out of bed. It was nearly ten o'clock. He couldn't believe that Douglas and Barbara had let him sleep in so long. He quickly dressed and made the bed. After tidying up the room, he headed out to the kitchen.

The smell of freshly brewed coffee greeted him when he walked around the corner into the dining room. Barbara was washing dishes by hand in the sink, but Douglas was nowhere to be seen.

"Morning sleepy head," she said, smiling over her shoulder at him while she continued to rinse a glass.

"I'm sorry I slept so late."

"No worries. It's Sunday, a day of rest," she said. "And I have to hurry or I'll be late for Mass." She wiped her hands on a small towel that hung from the handle of the dishwasher. Slipping off the apron, Harrison realized for the first time that she was wearing a dress and had her hair and make-up done.

"You look nice," he commented.

"Can't go to church looking like a slob. Only the best

for our Lord," she said. "Douglas is out back feeding the chickens. I should be home in an hour or so. Depends on whether Father Betts is saying the Mass or Father Glenn. Father Betts keeps it short. Father Glenn likes to hear himself talk, if you know what I mean." She smiled and gave him a wink.

"Yeah, I do," Harrison answered but really he didn't. He hadn't been to a church since the day he and Danika buried their father. The priest refused to let them have a church funeral claiming their father used alcohol to commit suicide and suicide was a mortal sin. Since then, Harrison hadn't really thought about God. It wasn't that he blamed God; he blamed the priest. It was just that he was too busy doing what had to be done to survive.

"Well, see you," Barbara called and closed the front door behind her.

Harrison took a coffee mug from the cupboard and helped himself to the coffee. He sat down at the table and stared out at the side yard. It was quiet and peaceful there. Harrison was alone with only his thoughts.

Danika's words were the first thing that came to his mind. *Don't you see, you've found someone else to mother.*

"No, I haven't," he whispered aloud and shook his head.

While he continued to sip his coffee, he thought about the day he met Thomas. He had just gone down to the first floor to get his lunch. While he stood in line, a young man approached him.

"Can you spare some change?" he asked.

"For?"

"I'm hungry and a little short on funds," he answered.

Harrison gave him the once over. The man didn't look like a bum. He was short, about five six or maybe seven, which made him look younger than his voice belied. He had dark brown, almost black, hair that was cut short on the sides and back but left long on the top in a sort of limp Mohawk style. His eyes were dark brown. He wore nice clothes, so his present situation probably wasn't a chronic one. All in all, he appeared to be a normal young man.

"I can do you better. Why don't you join me and I'll buy you lunch?"

The man turned his head and looked at Harrison. "I'm just looking for something to eat."

"That's okay."

"I'm not gay," he lowered his voice to a whisper.

"Me either," Harrison answered and glanced at his reflection in the darkened window of a nearby shop. *Why does everyone assume?* His gaze drifted to the young man's reflection. Harrison watched him give him the once over. Smiling, Harrison turned his head and gave the man an uncertain smile. "It's okay. It's just lunch."

"All right, sure," the man accepted.

While they ate, Harrison learned the young man's name, Thomas Unger. He was twenty-two, just out of UCLA. He had come to Portland in hopes of landing a job with Nike but they were taking their time in making a decision about his application, or so it seemed. In the meantime he had found odd jobs but those had dried up. He used the last of his money to pay the landlord to keep from being evicted from his studio apartment just a few blocks away.

"So have you applied for work anywhere else?" Harrison asked.

"Of course," Thomas answered while filling his mouth with rice and chicken. By the way he was eating, Harrison could tell he had missed quite a few meals. He began to feel sorry for the young man.

"But it's the same everywhere," Thomas continued and took a gulp of his cola. "We'll get back to you in two weeks. In two weeks I'll be on the street."

"What about your parents?"

"No. I can't go to them. They were against my moving here, away from their control. I'm their oldest and the first to leave home. They're way too possessive."

"I see," Harrison answered and glanced at his watch. "Say, I have to get back to work but," he took a card from his wallet, wrote on it and handed it to Thomas, "here's my number. If you ever need anything, a friend to talk to, or help, or anything, just call me."

Thomas took the card.

A few days later, while Harrison was head deep in paperwork at his desk, his cell phone rang. Harrison looked at the number and didn't recognize it but answered anyway.

"Hi, this is Thomas, Thomas Unger. We met last Tuesday."

"Oh, yes, I remember," Harrison answered. "How are you?"

"Not so great, I'm afraid. I'm being evicted."

"I thought you said you paid—" Harrison stopped himself. "Where are you?"

"I'm standing outside my apartment building on Salmon and Broadway."

Harrison looked at his watch. "Can you wait there for an hour? I'll be off work then and can drive over."

"Yeah, sure. It's not like I've anywhere to go," he said with a slight chuckle.

An hour later, Harrison parked his Bug in front of the old Sovereign Hotel that had been renovated into studio apartments again. Thomas stood leaning against the building with his foot resting on a large box. Another smaller box and suitcase were beside it.

"Hi," Harrison greeted and walked over to him.

"I'm sorry to call you, but I didn't have anyone else I could. You seemed nice."

"I take it you need a place to crash?"

Thomas nodded and looked embarrassed.

On the drive home, Harrison noticed Thomas was quite nervous. He kept apologizing for putting him on the spot.

"Nonsense," Harrison said. "I live alone in a three bedroom house with my cat, Col. Mustard—oh, you aren't allergic to cats are you?" Harrison asked and held his breath.

"No."

"Great." he sighed with relief. "You can stay for a week and we'll see how it goes."

"Okay, how much?"

"How—rent? I won't charge you. You just said you're having a rough time and have no money right now. Forget it. Maybe once you get a job we can talk about it again."

"Are you sure? That's being awfully nice to a stranger. You sure you don't want something?"

"Positive."

"No, no, I couldn't do that," Thomas said shaking his head.

"Yes, you can, really."

"But I don't know you. What if you're a serial killer or some deranged guy—"

"I guess you'll find out." Harrison said with an amused chuckle. "Look, I can afford it. The house is paid for; I inherited it when my parents died."

"Gee, I'm sorry," Thomas murmured.

"It's okay; it was a long time ago. Not to worry," Harrison assured him.

That was eight years ago. Harrison took another sip from his mug and realized he needed a refill. Just when he was putting the coffee pot back on the hotplate, the back door opened and Douglas walked into the dining room.

"Hey there, you're up," he said with a smile.

"Yeah, Barbara went off to church."

"I know. She goes every week when she's not working. I'll go get washed up and then we can head into town. That is if you still want to file that missing person report?"

"I do," Harrison answered with a nod. "Ready when you are."

Minutes later both men were in Douglas's work truck and heading down the driveway. Douglas stopped to look both ways when he reached the road.

"What's with the neighbor's car?" Harrison asked.

"What?" Douglas asked looking at the black car parked in the driveway across from them.

"I saw it yesterday when I went for a walk. It was parked there. Think it's for sale?"

"That's not the neighbor's car," Douglas said and pulled out on the road.

"It's not?" Harrison asked sounding surprised. He looked back over his shoulder. The black car pulled out onto the road and began following them. Harrison felt his pulse quicken. Too much had happened for it to be a coincidence that they were both leaving at the same time.

"I see it," Douglas said. His tone matched how Harrison felt inside.

While Douglas continued driving them toward

Ellensburg, Harrison kept an eye on the black car behind them. When they turned to cross the bridge, it turned with them. When Douglas took a detour, it followed.

"We'll see what it does when we pull into the police station," Douglas said, glancing into the side mirror.

They parked near the main entrance. As they climbed out of the cab, Harrison spotted the car. It had been parked against the curb across the side street. Instead of feeling afraid, Harrison started to feel his anger rise. He started toward the car.

"What are you doing?" Douglas asked.

"I've had enough of this," Harrison answered over his shoulder.

"That's not them," Douglas blurted, halting Harrison as he reached the sidewalk.

Harrison turned around. "What?"

"The car that was following us drove on," Douglas answered. "Come on, let's go inside."

The officer behind the counter entered the information Harrison gave her into a computer. When she was finished she assured Harrison the department would do everything they could to find Thomas. Still, Harrison couldn't deny the feeling that she had only repeated what she had been taught to say in some training class. There was no sense of sympathy or empathy in her tone, just a cold, mechanical, response.

When the two men left the building, Harrison spotted a Cadillac turning into the employee parking lot.

"Hey, can you do me a favor?" he asked, grabbing Douglas's arm.

"What?"

"Can you keep Chief Hanks busy? I want to check the VIN numbers on his cad." Harrison pulled the slip of paper from the pocket in his jeans.

"I don't know?" Douglas hesitated. "What would we talk about?"

"Ask him about Rosa? Ask him about, whatever," Harrison answered. "You know the man. I don't."

"Okay, but be careful." Douglas warned.

Harrison nodded and then slipped around the corner of the building. The parking lot was deserted. Only a handful of cars were there and the Cadillac was parked in a space reserved for the chief.

Cautiously Harrison approached, looking around to be sure it was clear. He walked up to the driver's side and with the paper securely palmed he glanced at the VIN plate. Slowly he read off the numbers and checked them against the paper. The numbers didn't match. Harrison felt his chest deflate. He stuffed the paper back into his pocket and turned around.

"Hey, you there!" a deep voice shouted.

Harrison froze. A burly policeman hurried across the lot toward him, his hand over his holster. Harrison raised his hands in mock surrender.

"What are you doing here?" he asked when they came face to face.

"Nothing. I was just admiring the Caddy."

"Yeah, well, this lot is restricted property and off limits to the public."

"I'm sorry. I didn't realize. I was passing by and caught a glimpse of the Caddy and had to take a closer look. You don't see many in this cherry condition around here. Is she yours?" Harrison glanced at the small nameplate above the officer's right breast pocket, "Sgt. H. Hathaway".

"Nah, it's the chief's," the sergeant shrugged and relaxed.

Harrison lowered his hands. "Wow, he keeps her looking great. How long's he had her?" He took a step back to pretend to admire it.

"About a week."

"A week? Is that all?"

"Yeah, he bought it out of the impound lot. Guess the previous owner didn't want it."

"I can't imagine anyone not wanting a classic like this especially in this condition. Look," Harrison bent down and looked through the driver's window. "The leather seats look original and are still in excellent condition." Suddenly he spotted a familiar chip. He felt his hands begin to tremble. *This is Thomas' car,* his thoughts shouted so loudly in his head that he was sure the officer could hear them. He looked at the policeman crouched down beside him.

"Nice," Hathaway murmured.

"Well, I should be going. I'm really sorry about the restricted property thing and all. It won't happen again."

"No problem," Hathaway answered and stood up.

Harrison had to force himself to keep from running as he quickly walked back to the sidewalk and headed toward the highway. When he was out of the sight of the cop, he rushed over to the truck and climbed into the passenger seat. Moments later, Douglas appeared. He climbed into the cab and started the truck.

"How did it go in there?" Harrison asked.

"Fine. I asked him about the black car. He said he doesn't know anything about it. Thought it could have been a coincidence. What about you?"

"It's Thomas' car all right. I don't know how they managed to change the VIN numbers but I could still tell it was his."

"How?" Douglas glanced at him before pulling back onto the highway.

"There is a chip in the corner of the fake wood paneling in the passenger door. It's where it comes to a point."

"How could you be sure?"

"Because I did it. Thomas was nice about it but I could tell he was upset. I still have the piece back home. I was going to glue it back on when I had the chance, but Thomas left on this trip."

"I—" Douglas's cell phone rang, interrupting him. "Hi, sweetheart, you home?" he answered the call. "No, we're in town heading back home." He glanced at Harrison and mouthed the name Barbara to him. Harrison nodded. "Okay, we'll meet you there." He disconnected and stuffed the phone back into his pocket. "She's through with church and wants to meet us at the Port Hole for lunch. She said she has some new information."

"Sounds good."

The Port Hole was packed. Church-goers, Douglas whispered over his shoulder. The noise from all the talking combined with the music made it hard to hear. Harrison wondered if this was a good idea. With all of these people, someone was bound to overhear them.

"We have a table right this way," the hostess said. She grabbed three menus from her station and led the two men to a table near the bar. "Sorry, it's so loud in here, but we're getting slammed."

"No worries," Douglas assured her. "This is fine."

Harrison glanced at the men seated at the bar just as one elbowed the other and they both looked at him. He smiled at them, ignoring the creeped out feeling inside, and sat down. The men turned away and continued talking.

"Those men at the bar," Harrison said leaning across the table toward Douglas. "They were here the day Rosa came in."

Douglas glanced over his shoulder at the men. "Yeah, they're regulars here. They run a fishing boat and a shuttle service taking fishermen back and forth to the big fishing boats that can't come into port."

"Interesting," Harrison said.

"Sorry, I'm late," Barbara appeared out of the crowd. She kissed Douglas on the cheek and sat down between the two men.

"How was church?" Harrison asked.

"It was fine. Father Glenn offered it and didn't disappoint when it came time for his sermon. He preached about the importance of donations and how they fund the different projects the Church is working on. I didn't pay too much attention frankly. I hate it when he does uses his time to solicit money instead of teach us about the Bible."

Harrison nodded and looked at the table, silently wishing he hadn't asked.

"After all, they are supposed to know what it says. They need to help us understand God's Word."

"True," Douglas interrupted. "So what did you find out?"

"Let's order first and then I'll tell you."

It took a while but eventually the waitress dressed as a wench came over and took their order. She returned moments later with their coffee and sodas.

"If you need anything else, just let me know." She smiled before leaving them.

"Okay, so what's up?" Douglas asked.

"I ran into Rene at church. She's the assistant medical examiner," she explained to Harrison. "I asked her about the

Rosa. At first she didn't want to say anything. She seemed quite upset, but then her work persona kicked in. She told me she had never seen such a brutal murder victim here. Rosa was stabbed repeatedly; the blade of the knife actually broke off inside her but she was still alive. The intruder then smashed Rosa's head into the toilet. That is what killed her."

"So, the break in was real?" Harrison asked.

"It seems so," Barbara answered and nodded. "But, no tweaked out druggie would have done this. This was too calculated; the stab wounds, too precise. No, this was more of a hit, in my opinion."

"Did Rene agree?"

"She did. She knew of Rosa. Her son goes to school with the Rosa's. The boys are friends and have spent time at each other's house many times. Rene's not sure how she's going to break the news to her son."

"That's gotta be rough," Douglas spoke up. "Has anyone heard if the police are investigating?"

Barbara shook her head and shrugged. "Too early for word to get out, but I'll keep my ears open."

"My money is on that police chief," Harrison spat.

"What about the police chief," Judd asked.

Harrison felt his whole body go tense. His mouth gaped open and he reached for his water glass but quickly took back his shaking hand.

"Nothing," Douglas answered. "We were just talking about our nice visit this morning."

"Well, I'm here to speak with your friend," he looked at Harrison.

Harrison's breath caught for a moment. He looked at Judd who had a pasted-on smile.

"I hear you were snooping around my car this morning,"

he said.

"I was admiring it," Harrison said, trying not to let his voice quiver like his legs and hands beneath the table.

"Well, may I make a suggestion, mind your own business. In fact, why don't you just move along down the road."

"You mean, get out of town?" Harrison's voice started to find its strength.

"Now, I would never try to discourage visitors to our fine town but you're looking for a friend of yours aren't you? Perhaps you should keep looking elsewhere."

"Find my car and I will." Harrison's anger took over.

Judd leaned closer. "You really don't want to push me. I'm not suggesting you leave. Catch my meaning?"

"Like I said, find my car and I will be happy to get out of this hick town," Harrison snapped.

Judd stood up sharply. His face was red and his teeth, clenched. "This is your last warning. Next time we meet, I won't be as nice." He turned around and left along with the other officer who had stood back. Harrison recognized him. He was Sergeant Hathaway, the one who caught him looking at the Cadillac.

As soon as the two cops were gone, Barbara put her hand over Harrison's.

"That was interesting," she said.

"I'll say," Douglas added with a note of laughter in his tone. "You sure have a lot of guts, Harry."

"Not really," Harrison said and held up his shaking hands. The three laughed.

CHAPTER TEN

Harrison woke with a splitting headache. He heard voices in the kitchen and looked at the window. It was still dark outside. He threw the covers off and slowly climbed out of bed. After putting on his clothes, he went to the kitchen in the hope that a cup of coffee would ease his pain.

"Morning," Barbara greeted in her usual cheery tone.

Harrison squinted, his head throbbing and ears ringing. He didn't remember how many bottles of beer he drank the night before but seeing at least a dozen empty bottles on the counter, he knew it had been too many.

"Here," Barbara smiled and handed him a cup of coffee. "This might help."

"What time is it?" he asked.

"It's six-thirty."

Harrison retreated to the table and sat down while Barbara continued tidying the kitchen and filling her thermos.

"I thought I heard Douglas?"

"You did. He had to get an early start so he said he would meet you later for lunch."

"Okay," Harrison nodded. "Say, are you going into town?"

"Yes. I have to be to work in an hour. Why?"

"Could I get a ride with you? I want to do some looking around."

"Do you think that's a wise idea?" Barbara leaned against the counter and dried her hands on a kitchen towel. "I mean after Judd's warning and all."

"I don't care about that. He doesn't scare me."

"I don't know about that, you were shaking pretty good..." she laughed.

"Well, maybe a little, but I do that when I get mad too, and he really pissed me off. Sorry."

"No problem. He has that effect on a lot of people. Sure, I'll give you a lift, but you have to promise to be careful."

"I promise." Harrison agreed.

After two more cups of coffee, Harrison's headache subsided. He ate a couple slices of toast with some of Barbara's homemade blackberry jam. It was just enough to take the edge off his morning hunger.

"Thank you again for letting me ride into town with you," Harrison said for the umpteenth time that morning.

Barbara didn't acknowledge it this time. She slowly drove down the driveway toward the street. When she reached it, she stopped and looked both ways.

Harrison felt all the warmth drain from his body when he noticed the black car parked across the street in the neighbor's driveway. He didn't say a word to Barbara, didn't want to cause her any alarm. He watched in the side mirror as the car began to follow them. He took a deep breath and let it out slowly.

"So, don't forget to give Douglas a call. Maybe you and

he could try Granny's for lunch. I hear they have great omelets and country fried potatoes."

"Sounds good."

"Plus, they aren't as busy as the Port Hole these days. They mostly cater to tourists and there aren't that many this time of year."

"I see," Harrison said and took another glance in the mirror. The car was still tailing them.

Barbara slowed her SUV and pulled into the parking lot of McKay's Grocery.

"I'm going to let you out here. The fire station is behind the police station. I don't think it is a good idea for you to get out there."

"Good call," Harrison said. When she brought the car to a stop, he opened the door and stepped out.

"Please be careful," she said and frowned at him.

"I will. I promised, remember?" He smiled at her.

She nodded and he shut the door.

Harrison stood for a moment and watched her drive away. He pulled out the photos of Thomas and the Cadillac and looked at them.

"Where are you?" he said aloud to himself. Sticking the photos back into his shirt pocket, he looked across the parking lot and froze. Parked across the street was the black car. He strained his eyes to see who was inside but saw no one. "Relax," he told himself, "there are a million black cars. Stop being paranoid." He turned around and headed into the store hoping there was a Starbucks inside or at least a coffee vendor.

Just when he was crossing the parking lot, nearing the doors, his cell phone rang. He took it out of his pocket and looked at the display. He didn't recognize the number but decided to answer it.

"Hello?"

"Harrison."

He recognized the voice. His conversation with Justus came back to him. "What do you want, Eric? I thought you said you didn't want to hear from me for two weeks."

"Ah, forget all that. I need you back in the office today."

"Not happening."

"Wha—" Eric's voice registered shock and disbelief.

Harrison grinned and tried not to laugh. It was probably the first time in his life that someone had told him no, Harrison thought.

"Can't make it. In fact, I won't be back for another week."

"But—"

"You suspended me, Eric, remember?"

"Yeah, well, I may have overreacted a bit. The clients never saw the reports. No harm was actually done."

"Really?" Harrison didn't even try to hide his sarcasm.

"Yes," Eric snipped. "I need you back here right away." His tone was demanding.

"Wish I could but I can't. I'm in Ellensburg."

"You're out of the country?"

Harrison rolled his eyes and shook his head. "No. I'm on the coast, thirty minutes from the California border. I'm looking for my friend, remember?"

"Oh, yeah."

"Since I've been suspended for two weeks without pay—"

"Well, about that, you will be paid for your time away."

"I'm not using my vacation time—"

"Oh, no," Eric interrupted. "It's all taken care of but I really need you to come back as soon as possible."

"At the end of two weeks, I will be back in the office but not until then."

"But…okay," Eric relented. "See you then."

Harrison tapped the "End" icon on his phone and stuck it back into his pocket. At that moment he was thankful he had spoken to Justus who gave him a head's up about the office politics. It gave him the confidence to stay firm with his young boss. He couldn't help gloating a bit while he continued on his way into the store.

Even though grocery stores tended to look the same, aisles of shelves filled with boxes and cans of food, tables of fresh produce, tall freezers with processed frozen pizzas, there was something different about the feel of this store. It screamed small town, mom and pop. Luckily, for Harrison, it wasn't too small town. He found a kiosk near the front doors that was serving freshly brewed specialty coffees. He stepped up and placed his order.

The barista appeared extremely young, as though she should still be in high school. She had her long, brown ponytail pulled through the back loop of her black baseball cap.

"So, how's your morning going?" she asked, making small talk while she brewed his coffee.

"Not bad," Harrison answered. He took out the photo in his pocket and looked around. It was still early and the store didn't appear to be busy.

"Here you go," the barista said and set his paper cup of coffee on the counter in front of him.

"May I ask you a question?" Harrison said trying to be polite and aware that she was working.

"Sure." She smiled at him.

"Have you seen this man?" He held up the photo.

126

The young girl looked at the photo and started to shake her head slowly. "No, I haven't. He's cute, though. I would have remembered him. Why are you looking for him? Did he do something wrong?"

"No," Harrison answered and put the photo back in his pocket. "He's a friend of mine and has gone missing."

"I'm sorry. I hope you find him, then."

Harrison smiled at the girl, took his coffee and left the store. While he walked across the parking lot toward Highway 101 that ran through the center of town he sipped his drink. Surprised, he smiled again and thought, for such a young girl, she made an excellent cup of coffee.

Reaching the sidewalk, he stopped. The black car was still parked against the curb. Again the urge to cross the highway and demand to know what the driver wanted, swelled in his chest along with his anger. In his imagination he saw himself, fists clenched, banging on the driver's window. As the tinted glass slowly sank into the door, he could see the grinning face of Judd Hanks.

"What do you want?" he would demand of the cop.

Before he could answer, Harrison was brought back to reality by the sight of a woman running up to the passenger side of the black car. She opened the door and climbed in. Slowly the car pulled away from the curb and was gone.

Harrison laughed at himself and took another sip of his morning coffee.

"Relax," he said out loud to himself.

He turned and began walking south, not sure where to start his search. While he walked he reviewed what he knew. Thomas had no car. He disappeared from the Ocean Front Inn the night he checked into it. Maybe he was still in town? Maybe he was hurt?

At the corner of 4th Street, Harrison noticed the blue sign with a large white H and an arrow pointing east. He crossed the highway and headed up the side street toward the hospital.

The brick façade of the building resembled an elementary school more than a hospital, Harrison thought. He walked into the lobby and approached the front desk. The older gentleman looked up and smiled. A nameplate on his left shirt pocket read, Volunteer.

"How may I help you?" he asked.

"I was wondering if you have a room number for Thomas Unger?" Harrison asked.

"Just a moment," the man answered and typed into his computer. "Let me see…"

Harrison wasn't sure what he felt. He wanted to find Thomas but dreaded the thought that he was injured or sick and alone in a hospital.

"I'm sorry, I don't show a room for him. When was he brought in?" the man interrupted Harrison's thoughts.

"I'm not sure if he was. You see, I'm looking for him." He pulled Thomas' photo out and showed it to the volunteer. "This is Thomas. He went missing from the Ocean Front Inn nearly two weeks ago."

The man looked at the photograph. He shook his head. "What a shame. I haven't seen him. Maybe he left town?"

"No," Harrison answered, putting the photograph back into his pocket. "His car broke down just north of town and I've seen it in town."

"Well, there you are. Where's his car?"

"The police chief is driving it."

The cheerful expression on the man's face drained away. "I'm sorry, I can't help you," he said in a formal business-like tone.

Harrison hesitated for a moment, bewildered by the sudden change in the man's voice.

"Okay," he said finally. "Thank you, anyway." He turned and walked back out to the street.

There was a sense of relief that he hadn't found Thomas in the hospital but at the same time Harrison felt disheartened that he was no closer to finding his friend. Lost in his thoughts and not paying attention to direction, Harrison looked around and realized that he didn't know where he was. He looked at the sky but the sun was too high for him to tell direction. To his left was a forest, to his right, what appeared to be an elementary school's playground and sports field.

"Great!" he said out loud. "You've gone and got yourself lost. What an idiot you are."

"Who you talkin' to?" a tiny voice asked.

Harrison jumped and looked at the trees. There, standing beside the thick trunk of an old oak tree was a little girl. She wore a dirty, tattered dress with patches sewn here and there. Her long, brown hair fell in ringlets around her small shoulders and was in need of a good washing and brushing. Her cheeks and legs were dirty and she wore no shoes despite it being cool out.

"Shouldn't you be school?" he asked.

She shook her head. "I don't go to school," she said with a note of sadness in her voice.

"Why not? I thought that all little boys and girls your age went to school."

"'cause mama says I don't need book learnin'."

Harrison frowned. "My name is Harrison. What's yours?"

"Serenity," she answered and tilted her head coyly to one side while she tugged on her tattered dress.

129

"That's a pretty name. How old are you?"

"Eight an' a half," she answered proudly, puffing up her tiny chest. "Who you talkin' to a minute ago?" she asked.

"I was talking to myself."

"Why?"

"Because I was thinking about my friend and not paying attention to where I was going and now I'm lost."

"Who's your friend?"

Harrison pulled the photo from his pocket and held it out to the little girl.

Cautiously she crept out to the side of the road to get a closer look.

"I seen him," she said excitedly.

Harrison felt a sudden jolt in his chest. "You have? Where?"

"In the woods," she looked over her shoulder and pointed.

"Where in the woods?"

"A long ways away. He and some men were all in the woods."

"Can you show me?"

Just then the school bell rang and children poured out of the building. Serenity took one look at them and turned around. Before Harrison could stop her, she dashed back into the forest and disappeared. He thought about chasing after her but decided it wouldn't do him any good getting further lost. He turned around and froze.

The blue and red strobe lights flashed on the roof of the squad car. The driver's door opened and a policeman stepped out, his right hand on his holster, his left hand held out showing his palm to Harrison.

"Hold it right there! Put your hands on your head." he

barked.

Harrison raised his hands and complied.

"Turn around and face away," the officer ordered.

Again Harrison complied. Instantly he felt the metal of the handcuffs grab his right wrist and pull it behind his back. The officer then took hold of Harrison's left wrist and pulled it back, locking the cuff securely around it.

"What have I done?" Harrison asked while the officer led him back to his squad car.

"We got a report about a man lurking around the playground."

"I wasn't lurking. I was out walking and got lost," Harrison tried to explain.

"The report said the man was trying to lure a child into the woods."

"No, I wasn't. The little girl came out of the woods and talked to me."

"Yeah, so typical, blame the innocent children. I know your kind. You make me sick. Get in and watch your head."

"You've got this all wrong."

The officer shoved Harrison into the back seat and slammed the door. Moments later they pulled into the police station just a half a mile away. Harrison was led into the building, to a small room with a table and three chairs in the center.

"Sit here," the officer ordered and cuffed Harrison's wrists to the table. "I'll be right back."

Before Harrison had a chance to think about his situation, the door to the room opened again and in walked Chief Hanks. He closed the door behind him.

"Didn't take my warning seriously, I see," he said in a stern but condescending tone.

"I don't have a car," Harrison answered with all the venom he could muster.

Without warning, Chief Hanks backhanded Harrison across the face. Harrison's head turned sharply with the blow. His cheek stung, his ears rang, and his neck muscles hurt.

"What was that for?"

"Don't get smart with me. When I order someone out of my town, I expect them to obey." He continued to pace around the room.

"Where's my car? Where's my friend?" Harrison demanded.

Again, a sharp blow. More pain. He could taste blood in his mouth but didn't dare spit.

"What car? What friend?" Judd sneered leaning forward with his fists pressing onto the top of the table.

Harrison could feel the heat from the police chief's putrid breath. He turned his head away and tried not to gag.

"What's this?" the chief said, pulling the photographs out of Harrison's pocket. "Is this your friend?" he asked and then his eyes widened for a moment before narrowing into thin slits. Slowly he tore the photographs into tiny fragments. He leaned across the table until his face was just inches from Harrison. "I want you out of my town," he seethed. "Can you do that?"

"Once I get a rental car, I'll be gone." Harrison knew that was a lie before he even said it, but he had to get out of there. Being locked up wasn't going to help him find Thomas any faster and it sounded as though the Chief would let him go if he agreed to leave town.

"I will give you twenty-four hours. If you're still here after that, I'll haul your ass back in here and make you regret not heeding my recommendation."

Harrison nodded.

By the time Harrison reached Granny's, the pain in his head had centered on his cheek and radiated down to his jaw. He put his hand to his face but feared touching it. He wasn't in the mood for lunch but was anxious to see Douglas.

The restaurant wasn't busy. A few diners sat in clusters scattered around the open dining room. Just inside the front door was the hostess station that resembled a podium. A sign painted on the front told diners to wait to be seated. A young girl approached. Harrison watched her smile fade.

"Welcome to Granny's, are you okay, sir?" she asked, her eyes showing concern.

"Yes, why?"

"Perhaps you want to go in the restroom and check yourself?" she said. The look in her blue eyes made Harrison worried.

"Sure," he answered her. "That would be great."

The hostess showed him to the back of the restaurant where the restrooms were located.

"I'll have your table ready when you come out," she said. "And I'll get some ice for that eye."

"That would be great. Could I get one away from other diners, please?"

"Most definitely," she answered and smiled.

Harrison walked into the restroom. It was clean and smelled of men's cologne. He walked over to the sink and looked at his reflection in the mirror. His breath caught for a moment when he saw his face. His left eye was bruised and swollen nearly shut. His cheek down to his jaw was red and scratched. Harrison remembered the large, rough, gold nugget rings on Judd's stubby little fingers and cursed him under his breath. Harrison's lip was split near the corner of his mouth and was smeared with dried blood. He knew he was hurt but hadn't known how bad he looked.

Harrison turned the water on in the sink and washed his face. He took a couple paper towels and gently dabbed himself dry. The bruise was still there but the blood was gone. With a deep breath, he walked out of the restroom.

The hostess handed him a plastic bag of ice wrapped in a cloth napkin and then showed him to a table away from the others, in a quieter corner of the dining room. After Harrison informed her that he was waiting for a friend, she brought another menu and glass of ice water. While he waited for Douglas, he sipped on his water and held the ice pack to his cheek. It stung at first but soon his face numbed.

At about twenty after one Douglas walked through the front door. He spotted Harrison in the corner and informed the hostess, who escorted him to the table.

"What the devil happened to you?" Douglas asked.

Harrison recounted the morning he'd had, his getting lost and finding Serenity and about his run in with Chief Hanks. His excitement about learning Thomas had been seen overshadowed his pain and the threats made by the Chief. "Do you know anything about the woods near an elementary school?"

"Just that they're huge and cover from the edge of town west past the Hanks' property. If he's in there, it could take months to find him, years if it's just the two of us. We need help. Do you think that girl could help us?"

"No. She ran back into the woods before I could find out anymore."

"Too bad," Douglas said and shook his head.

"Are you ready to order?" the waitress asked when she walked up to them.

CHAPTER ELEVEN

Harrison woke with a splitting headache. He looked at the clock. It was barely six in the morning. The house was quiet. He figured Douglas was still asleep upstairs. Throwing the blankets aside, Harrison sat up on the edge of the bed. He gingerly touched his cheek. It throbbed and was still sore. He made his way to the bathroom where he left his toiletry bag and retrieved his Advil. After taking two, he paused and took two more, then retreated back to the bedroom and dressed for the day. Douglas had agreed to take him to Coos Bay to get a rental car.

The coffee was just finished brewing when the front door opened and Barbara, still dressed in her EMT uniform walked in. She took a deep breath and smiled.

"Morning—what the devil happened to you?" she gasped. Her smile vanished.

"Long story," Harrison tried to smile but it felt more like a grimace.

"Let me take a look at that," she said and pulled a chair out from the table and pointed for him to sit. "Spill it."

While she examined the bruises and felt his cheek bones, Harrison filled her in on all that happened the day before.

"What a coincidence," she said when Harrison finished. "A week ago I was called out to a gypsy camp in the forest behind the Indian Creek Cafe. A young woman Memory was violently ill. Anyway, there was a little girl there by the name of Serenity. I remember because she had the most beautiful, clear blue eyes and long, dark, curly hair."

"That's her!" Harrison nearly shouted. "Thank God. I was beginning to think I had imagined her, like those ghosts in movies that show up along country roads in the middle of nowhere. Can you take me their camp?"

"Yes, but it's quite a hike. It took my partner and me a good hour to get there and that was with the help from one of their members leading the way."

"Dang, now I wish I could put off going to Coos Bay." Harrison slumped in his chair.

"I can show you tomorrow."

While Barbara started breakfast, Harrison went outside to get some fresh air. He stood on the front porch and leaned against the rail. The cool morning air smelled clean and felt good against his cheeks. He took a deep breath and pulled out his cell phone. He dialed Danika's number.

"Hello, Harry," she sounded wide awake.

"Hi, Dani. You busy? Can you talk?"

"I'm getting ready to go into court, what's up?"

"A lot. How much time can you spare?"

"About five minutes," she answered.

"Well, maybe—"

"Just tell me the Reader's Digest version," she said sounding exasperated.

"Okay." Harrison briefly reviewed the events of the last two days.

"Harry, did anyone witness the police chief hit you?"

"No. He kept the other officer out of the room."

"Damn. It's just your word against his," she answered. "If he should ever pick you up again, don't say a word except you want a lawyer. Then call me. I'll find you an honest one."

"Okay."

"And about that gypsy camp, be careful. They have their own set of rules, their own laws. Don't go there alone."

"I won't."

"Good, well, I've got to go. I'll do some checking to see what can be done about that cop. He can't go around assaulting people."

"Okay."

"Bye for now."

Danika disconnected the call. Harrison stared at his phone for a moment and then stuck it back in his pocket. He wished he could have talked to her more but understood she was in a hurry.

Two hours later, Harrison and Douglas said their good-byes to Barbara who was off to bed for a much needed nap. "Working twenty-four hours straight takes its toll," she reminded them. "It's not just sitting around playing cards all day and night. People do get into trouble and usually after the sun goes down." She smiled when she said it, and even though they only met a few days ago, Harrison could see in her eyes that she cared about the people she helped.

Sitting in the passenger seat of Douglas's work truck on the way to Coos Bay, Harrison looked out the window and let his mind wander back to the day Thomas landed his dream job.

Thomas was so excited. He phoned Harrison at work

three times to be sure Harrison was coming straight home. Harrison finally told him he needed to get work done or he would have to stay late. When he arrived at home, Thomas was waiting for him on the front steps, grinning from ear to ear.

"Guess who landed a job at Nike?" he asked.

"Oh, let me take a stab in the dark, Col. Mustard?" Harrison teased.

"Very funny."

"Congratulations, Thom. I'm really proud of you for not giving up on your dream. When do you start?"

"Monday," Thomas answered. "Now I can finally start paying you back for all that you've done for me."

"There's no need. Save your money for you."

Thomas shook his head. "No, I've been living off you for the past eight months. I don't want money to ruin our friendship."

"It's not, unless you insist on paying me back," Harrison twisted the conversation.

"Not fair. I don't have an attorney for a sister."

"What's Dani got to do with this?"

"Nothing, never mind, but this discussion is not over. I'll figure out something." Thomas grinned but squinted which told Harrison he was in for a surprise.

Sure enough, after Thomas had received his first paycheck, the first thing he bought was a gift certificate to Nike for Harrison. The gift made Harrison feel uncomfortable and yet happy at the same time. He wasn't used to receiving gifts or even a thank you and it felt awkward.

Douglas hit the brakes, jolting Harrison out of his thoughts and back to the present. He grabbed the dashboard to brace himself. The tires squealed in protest as the truck went from fifty-five to a near crawl, narrowly missing rear-ending the car in front of them.

"What the hell?" Douglas shouted.

Harrison craned his neck to see in front of the car. There was nothing there. No reason for the driver to be moving so slow.

"Freaking tourists!" Douglas cursed.

Harrison looked in the side mirror to see if anyone was behind them. His breath caught when he saw the black car.

"How long have they been following us?" he asked, hating the note of fear he heard in his voice.

Douglas looked in his mirrors and shook his head. "I don't know. What's it matter?"

"It's that black car—"

"It's *a* black car, Harry. There are millions of them. Don't be so paranoid."

Harrison looked again. The driver put his turn signal on and turned off the highway and onto a side street. Harrison relaxed and felt slightly embarrassed.

"See, they weren't following us. They just happen to be going in the same direction is all," Doug said with a shrug. Suddenly he smacked the steering wheel with the palm of his hand. "Come on! Put your damned foot on the gas pedal and press it down!" he shouted through the windshield.

Harrison tried not to laugh.

When they reached Bandon, the slow poke turned off and Douglas sped up.

"Careful, there's a speed limit," Harrison warned.

Douglas eased up on the gas.

They arrived in Coo Bay at straight up noon. The streets were congested with the lunch crowd as well as the through traffic.

"You wanna get some lunch before we pick up your rental?" Douglas asked.

"Sure, why not." Harrison answered.

Douglas pulled into the parking lot of Abby's Pizza. He parked near the entrance and shut off the motor.

"Don't tell Barbara, but every time I have to come to Coos Bay for work, I have lunch here."

"Why's that a secret?"

"She says all that sodium and grease is a heart attack waiting to happen," Douglas said and smiled.

"I see," Harrison said but really he didn't. A person had to eat something and this day and age everything seemed like it wasn't good for you depending on who you asked.

After ordering a medium Ultimate Meat Pizza and a couple beers, the two sat down at a table away from the noisy teenaged diners. They appeared to be a high school sports team, all dressed in the same colored hoodies. They were laughing and enjoying their lunch away from campus.

"So, once you get the rental, then what are your plans?" Douglas asked. "You aren't leaving are you?"

"Hell, no. I don't care what that stinking top cop says. I'm not leaving until I find Thomas. Plus, I'm not looking forward to going back to work. There's a woman in the office that's sleeping with the boss. She's making a lot of trouble for a lot of people. She's already had one gal fired."

Douglas shook his head. "I'm so glad not to have to deal with all of that drama. Down here, all my interaction is over the phone with the exception of an occasional trip to stock up on supplies. Plus, everyone here is so laid back, not wound up so tight they have to bother everyone else."

"Sounds good," Harrison said with a nod. "Still, you have that power happy little policeman to contend with. I don't think I could live in a town run by a crooked cop."

"That's why I live outside the city limits." Douglas laughed. "Besides, you don't think there are dirty cops in Portland?"

"If there are, I don't know about it and that's the point. Here, that guy is in your face—"

"Literally, in your case," Douglas interrupted and smirked.

Harrison couldn't help but laugh with him. For the first time since they left the house, he became aware of how sensitive his bruised cheek was.

Their pizza arrived and the tomato sauce served as an even stronger reminder that being smacked around wasn't a memory he'd soon be able to forget. Hunger overcame the pain though and while the two ate they laughed and reminisced about their high school days and how things had changed.

"When we were in school, no one was allowed to leave campus without permission from their parents," Harrison recalled.

They watched the teens leave and saw the destruction they left behind. Used napkins littered the floor, plates of half-eaten pizza crust and lettuce from overflowing salads covered the tables. Even a few chairs were knocked over and left where they fell.

"We would have been in so much trouble if we did that," Douglas said and shook his head.

"We did and worse," Harrison laughed. "Remember that one time you, Jack, me and…oh what was his name?"

"Eldon."

"Yeah, that's him. We had gone out for pizza after watching a movie. Eldon wanted a souvenir and decided to swipe a mug. He stood up and put on his coat, wrapping it around the mug. Somehow, with his hands in his pockets, he managed to hold it."

"Yeah, right," Douglas scoffed. "Until we were standing at the counter, paying. That mug slipped out from under his coat and shattered on the floor."

"I still remember the owner's face. Good thing he only made Eldon pay for the mug after he cleaned it up instead of calling the police," Harrison said and leaned back in his chair. "Those were great times."

Douglas nodded.

The two were still laughing about their memories when they returned to the truck. The car rental office was twelve minutes away at the airport in North Bend.

It took no time at all for Harrison to secure a Volkswagen Jetta. He signed the necessary paperwork and paid with his credit card. It felt good to be behind the wheel of a car again, Harrison thought while he turned the key in the ignition. The car started up and he put it into gear. He followed while Douglas led the way back to Highway 101.

The trip down the coast to Ellensburg seemed to take longer, even though traffic was light and moving at the posted speed limit or above. It gave Harrison plenty of time to think and plan his next move.

Tomorrow he would get up. Barbara would show him where the gypsy camp was and they would get Serenity to show them where she saw Thomas. They would find him and bring him back to the house. Then he and Thomas would return home the following day. They could deal with their stolen cars from the safety and comfort of their home three hundred miles away.

Their home, Harrison's mind repeated. When had it become *their* home? True, it had been eight years since

Thomas had moved in and on paper the house was still Harrison's, but when did it become *theirs*? Harrison tried to remember but he couldn't pinpoint a specific date. It really doesn't matter, he told himself. What matters is finding Thomas and bringing him home safely.

"You've found someone else to mother," Danika's words flashed in his mind so loudly he could hear them.

"So what if I have?" Harrison said to the windshield. "Is that so terrible? You've got the boys. Why can't I help a friend?"

There was no reply.

Harrison focused his attention on the road ahead. He glanced at the sign "Entering Port Orford" and wished he hadn't. He slowed the Jetta to the proper speed. His pulse rate picked up the closer he drew to Hanks' Gas Station. Memories of stopping there flooded his mind along with the anxiety of knowing that was the place where everything started. Thomas had made the mistake of stopping there and then vanished. He had stopped there and had it not been for Douglas running into him alongside the road, would he have vanished too?

Harrison gripped the wheel and glanced at the gas station when he passed. Bubba was busy filling the tank of an old Ford while he appeared to be having a conversation with a man. An uneasy feeling formed in the pit of Harrison's stomach. He wanted to yell a warning to the guy but instead kept driving.

How long he had held his breath, Harrison couldn't say. He wasn't aware of it until he gasped for air.

"Damn it, relax!" he chastised himself. He rolled his window down to let the cool ocean air calm him. He took slow, deep breaths and the salty air did its job well.

When he came to the Humbug turns, Harrison slowed to

thirty-five. He glanced in the rear view mirror and suddenly his anxiety returned. A black sedan of unknown make was behind him, about three car lengths. The windows were tinted so he was unable to see the driver's face which was silhouetted by the light that shone through the back window. Harrison's pulse quickened. He sped up in an effort to put more distance between them. The sharp turns threatened to roll the Jetta as Harrison took them at nearly fifteen miles an hour over the posted limit.

Once through the turns, he glanced in the mirror again. The black car was still behind him and beginning to close the gap. Harrison pressed on the gas and sped up behind Douglas's truck. He waited for the oncoming lane to clear, then Harrison pulled over and passed Douglas. Once in the lead, Harrison slowed to sixty, just five miles over the posted limit. He glanced in his side mirror and saw the black car was passing Douglas. Harrison slowed and closed the gap between him and Douglas so the mystery driver would be forced to pass him as well.

His plan worked. When the car was beside Harrison he could feel the driver's eyes on him. The car pulled back into the southbound lane and stayed ahead of Harrison the rest of the way to Ellensburg.

Once they reached the bridge, the black car crossed it. Harrison turned left before the bridge and breathed a sigh of relief.

CHAPTER TWELVE

Harrison couldn't remember which he saw first when he reached the Blair's driveway, the flashing lights on the squad car that blocked the entrance or the rescue truck and ambulance parked along the side of the road. He slammed on the brakes. The gravel that covered the road caused the Jetta to fishtail. Harrison brought it to a safe stop and jumped from behind the wheel.

Douglas had pulled his truck up to the squad car and was already out and heading for the gate when Harrison caught up with him.

"What's—" the words caught in Douglas's throat and he froze. His whole body began to tremble. "Barbara!" he shouted.

Two county deputies rushed him and each grabbed an arm, holding him back.

"Let me go!" he yelled, twisting against their tight grasp.

"Mr. Blair, stop," one of the deputies holding him said softly but clearly.

Harrison felt his strength drain away when he saw the gate. The Blair's sign that had hung in the center of the cross beam with such pride was broken in two; half of it torn from its chain. A rope, looped around the beam, held Barbara suspended in midair. Harrison's trembling fingers scraped through his hair, then he covered his mouth with his hands, as if to stifle a scream.

A deputy, standing on hood of a county SUV, cut the rope that was tied around one of the upright posts. Slowly and carefully he lowered Barbara into the waiting arms of the EMTs.

Harrison looked at Douglas. He was still pushing against the two deputies but making no forward progress. "Let me go, god damn it!" he cursed and groaned. "No. Barbara!"

Harrison could feel Douglas's pain. He wanted to comfort his friend, but there was nothing he could do. Whether he broke free or the deputies finally released him, Harrison didn't know, but suddenly Douglas rushed forward to the gurney where Barbara lay.

The EMTs had just laid a sheet over her and were about to cover her face when Douglas grabbed it and tore it away.

"Don't you dare!" he growled at them. The two men raised their empty hands and stepped back. Douglas wrapped his arms around Barbara's limp body and pulled her into a hug while he sobbed. "Breathe, baby, breathe."

Harrison slowly walked closer and stood near the foot of the gurney. He looked at the house and saw a deputy approaching from that direction. He came down the driveway and put his hand on Douglas's back as though he knew him.

Harrison noticed that his badge said "Sheriff" and realized this was no deputy. This was the boss.

"Doug," Sheriff Porter spoke in a gentle tone. "Please,

let her go and let the EMTs take her. She's gone."

"No," Douglas groaned like a child while he sobbed.

"Please," the sheriff repeated. "You can't help her now. We were too late."

Slowly Douglas eased his grip on Barbara and laid her gently back on the gurney. He kissed her pallid cheek. "I'm so sorry, babe. I should have been here. I'm sorry."

Gently, Sheriff Porter pulled Douglas away and the EMTs resumed their duties.

Harrison stepped back and watched while they covered Barbara's face with the sheet. He noticed the bruises and scrapes on her cheeks. When he looked up, Doug and the sheriff were already heading for the house. Harrison took a step to follow but a deputy stepped in front of him.

"You'll need to stay back."

"But I'm staying here," Harrison protested.

Douglas stopped and turned back. "He's with me," he told the deputy.

The man hesitated for a moment and then stepped aside. Harrison quickly caught up with Douglas and the two followed the sheriff to the house.

"I have to—"

Just then Chief Hanks appeared in the front doorway.

"What's he doing in my house?" Douglas demanded, interrupting the sheriff.

"It's alright. He's helping me out with this."

"Like hell he is!"

"Doug, please," Sheriff Porter said stepping in front of him and putting his hand on Douglas's chest.

Chief Hanks walked out onto the porch and waited for the three men to join him.

"Frank," he spoke to the sheriff. "I'm afraid we have a

case of suicide."

Before anyone could stop him, Douglas threw a punch that struck the police chief in the jaw. Judd reeled back, lost his balance and crashed against the wall. Immediately Frank jumped between them. "Stop it!"

Douglas lunged but Harrison grabbed his arm. He turned to look at Harrison and the fight seemed to drain from him.

"You just assaulted a policeman," Judd barked and reached for his handcuffs.

"I think under the extenuating circumstances, we can overlook it, Judd," Frank insisted.

The chief glared at Douglas and slowly let go of his cuffs. "Seeing as how you're in shock and grief, I will let that one go. But you only get one free pass. Do it again and you will be sorry."

"Let's go inside," Frank said and moved Douglas toward the front door.

Douglas stepped into his home and stopped. His mouth dropped open while he looked around the living room.

Harrison couldn't believe what he saw. The room was trashed. The flat-screen TV in the corner was shattered. The sofa was askew and the coffee table lay in a broken heap in the center of the room.

"What have you done to my house," Douglas growled at the police chief. Harrison noticed Douglas's hands were clenched into tight fists.

"We did nothing. Your wife did this," Judd answered. "I've seen it before. High on meth or some other drug, she goes crazy and thrashes the place. When she starts to come down, she sees what she's done. Maybe she's even afraid of what you'd do to her. So, she decides to end it."

"Why you son-of-a—" Douglas growled through clenched teeth. His right fist drew back. Harrison grabbed it before it had a chance to find its intended target.

"Doug, stop it!" Harrison shouted while he struggled to restrain his friend.

"You don't know what you're talking about. You didn't know her. Barbara was a church going woman. She'd never get high." Douglas continued to struggle and pull against Harrison and Sheriff Porter's hold. His eyes narrowed in a burning rage.

Harrison couldn't blame Douglas for wanting to get another punch at Chief Hanks. Hell, he wanted to take a shot at him himself. The person Hanks had just described was nothing like the woman he had known for such a brief time. There was no way Barbara would have done any of this and she certainly would not take her own life. Her faith wouldn't allow it.

Harrison looked up at the loft and bedroom door at the top of the stairs. The door was open but from where he stood, Harrison couldn't see into the room. His eyes followed the stairs down to the floor under his feet. The wood flooring was oddly clean for so many law enforcement people going in and out. He looked at the baseboard and felt a shudder ripple through him. There was something red in caulking. Harrison looking into the living room at the sofa again that had been pulled away from the stairs. Craning his neck a bit, he glanced behind it. On the floor between the back of sofa and the wall was a shotgun. His head jerked to the side, he looked at the television. The pieces were starting to fit together.

"Come over here and sit down," Frank instructed pulling Douglas through the living room toward the dining table.

Douglas obeyed and with every step away from Chief Hanks, his body seemed to relax and his hostility waned. Frank up righted a chair with his free hand and offered it to Douglas who obediently sat down. Once the sheriff let go of Douglas, Harrison did the same. He grabbed another chair and set it right. He sat down, facing the kitchen as usual but the sight was anything but normal. The cupboards appeared to have been emptied, their contents thrown around the room. Dishes and pans were scattered across the floor, some shattered. Harrison could not believe Barbara would have done this. No. Something else went on here.

"So you know that I'm not just making this up, one of my men found this," Judd said and held out a slip of paper to Frank.

"Where's the evidence bag?" Frank asked.

Judd looked at the paper in his hand. He shrugged indifferently and then called out to one of his men to bring him a plastic bag. Once the paper was properly protected, he handed it to the sheriff.

"Where did you find this?"

"Upstairs."

"What were you doing upstairs?" Douglas challenged and started to rise out of his seat.

"We have to search the entire scene," Frank answered and put his hand on Douglas' shoulder, gently guiding him back down.

"What is it?" Douglas asked but it sounded like a demand.

"It's—"

Before Sheriff Porter could finish, Douglas snatched the paper from his hands and looked at it.

"This is bullshit!" he snapped. "This isn't hers. She

didn't write this. Besides, she would never kill herself. It's a mortal sin. Her soul would be damned to hell forever."

Frank took the paper back. "We'll have it looked at by an expert, Douglas. I assure you, until we get their results it won't be admitted as evidence."

"Just get him out of my house and out of my sight," Douglas said.

"Judd . . ." Frank said and nodded his head toward the front door.

"Okay," Chief Hanks said. "I just want to say, it's been my experience that the people closest to the deceased usually can't accept it facts that their loved one could kill—"

"Get out!" Douglas shouted and leapt from his chair. His entire body trembled but he didn't take a swing at the chief.

Judd hastily retreated and disappeared out the front door. The rest of his men inside the house quietly followed.

Slowly Douglas dropped back into his chair. His shoulders slumped and his head drooped down. Harrison could tell that Douglas was overwhelmed and was barely hanging on. He put his hand on Douglas's shoulder. This time instead of pulling away, Douglas leaned toward him. Harrison looked at the sheriff as though asking him how much longer.

"We're almost finished here," Frank assured them both. "Sit tight. I'll be right back."

Harrison watched the sheriff head outside. He stopped on the porch in plain sight of Harrison. Judd Hanks walked back into view and the two men talked in hushed voices

Douglas turned and looked at Harrison. "What am I going to do?"

Harrison saw the pain in his friend's eyes and the tears that dampened his cheeks.

It took three hours before the sheriff and his men left the premises. One of the deputies moved the truck and rental car, parking them in the driveway at the edge of the side yard, before he left. Once they were gone the house was eerily quiet.

Harrison headed to the living room. He moved the sofa back into place and noticed that the shotgun was missing. He didn't remember seeing who had taken it but he was sure it was now in the possession of the sheriff. He gathered up the broken pieces of wood that were once the coffee table and took them out to the front porch and piled them neatly there.

When he returned he noticed that Douglas had found a couple bottles of beer and was seated in his leather chair. He unscrewed the cap off one bottle and chugged it before reaching for the other.

It took Harrison almost an hour to clean up the mess in the kitchen. By then, the sun had already dipped below the horizon. He found a loaf of bread and some left-over meatloaf on the bottom shelf in the refrigerator and made a couple sandwiches. He put them on two unbroken plates he found in the dishwasher.

"Here," he spoke softly to Douglas, "you should eat something."

Douglas looked at him and took the plate. He set it on the small side-table next to his chair. "Got another beer?" he asked.

"I think so."

Harrison retrieved another bottle from the kitchen and a glass of red wine for himself. He handed the bottle to Douglas before he took a seat on the sofa.

"She didn't do this," Douglas spoke first. "She didn't..." He took a drink from his bottle.

"No, there is no way she would have," Harrison said

quietly.

"What were they looking for?" Douglas asked.

"I don't know. Maybe the laptop?"

Douglas looked at him. "Where is it?"

"I put it under the seat in your truck."

Douglas jumped to his feet and ran out to his truck. By the time Harrison reached the porch steps, Douglas was back, the laptop in his hand. For a moment they both stood looking at it. Harrison had a vision of Douglas throwing it across the lawn, smashing it beyond repair.

"Here," Douglas said and handed it to him. He pushed past Harrison and went back into the house.

When Harrison returned to the living room he found Douglas sitting on the floor and leaning his back against the sofa. He fumbled with the label on his half empty bottle of beer.

"Doug, I'm so sorry," Harrison said.

"About what?" Douglas looked at him.

"About this, Barbara, it's all my fault. If I hadn't come here—"

"Nonsense, this isn't your doing. But believe me, I will find out who did this and I will kill the son of a bitch."

Douglas took another drink from his bottle. Cautiously Harrison sat down on the floor next to his friend. He couldn't shake the guilt he felt and that it was his fault. He took another drink of wine from his glass.

"You want to know a secret?" Douglas asked while he peeled the label from his bottle.

"What?" Harrison asked trying not to sound too surprised by Douglas's question.

"I haven't been completely honest with you."

Harrison fought his initial response to look at Douglas.

Instead he kept focused on the wood burning stove across the room that sat between the two, dark windows. "What do you mean?"

"I didn't approach Barbara and ask her out after my accident. She looked me up." He took another long drink, emptying his bottle. "I had sworn off getting involved with anyone again after my previous entanglement. She pursued me."

"That's not so unusual these days."

"True, but . . ." he shook his head. "Is there anymore beer?"

"I'll check." Harrison jumped up and a moment later returned with another bottle. "Looks like this is the last one." He handed it to Douglas and sat back down.

Douglas unscrewed the cap and took a long drink.

"Can I ask you a favor?" he said sounding tired.

"Sure, what?"

"Just keep me company tonight. I don't want to go to bed."

"Sure," Harrison answered.

Douglas sat close to Harrison on the couch, as if the nearness of his friend gave him a measure of strength. They continued their conversation, pretending there was nothing new and horrible to be faced by thinking of the future. They reminisced about their childhood days, about days spent playing superheroes and building their secret lair. Those were carefree days where their biggest worry was being home in time for dinner. *When had life become so complicated?* Harrison thought.

Harrison didn't remember who fell asleep first, just that when he woke the next morning, Douglas was asleep, stretched out on the sofa with the throw blanket around him.

Quietly Harrison slipped into the kitchen and started a pot of coffee. He couldn't help but think about Barbara. He'd stepped into her routine and it was…disturbing. Peeking around the corner into the living room, he checked to make sure he hadn't disturbed Douglas. He was still fast asleep. Harrison decided to take a little walk outside to get some fresh air and clear his head.

Slipping out the back door, Harrison was hit by the damp, chilly, morning air. He wrapped his arms around himself and headed toward the front of the house. Just when he reached the driveway, he noticed someone standing by the gate looking up at the crossbeam.

"Good morning," he greeted the elderly man.

"Oh, 'morning," the man answered and frowned.

"I'm Harrison. I'm a friend of the Blair's." He held out his hand to the man.

"I'm Wallace. I'm the neighbor from across the street."

"Oh, you have the black car."

Wallace gave Harrison a confused look. "No," he said. "I drive an old Nissan pick-up, silver grey."

"I'm sorry. It's just that for the last few days I've seen a black car in your driveway."

Wallace turned and looked back at his property. "Haven't seen it," he said with a shrug of his aged and rounded shoulders. "Sad thing about what happened to Barbara."

"Yes, it is."

"How's Douglas doing?"

Harrison turned back toward the house. "He's sleeping right now. Do you know what happened here?"

"I can't say exactly. I was out back when I heard a shotgun go off. At first I couldn't tell where the sound came from but then I heard another. I came running down my driveway and I noticed a police car parked near the Blair's driveway. I figured they were there and handling whatever was going on. So, I went back to my business."

"A police car? The sheriff?"

"No, no, the Ellensburg Police."

Harrison turned and looked again at the house in the distance.

"Did you see anyone or anything else?"

"No, like I said, I went back to mending my fence. It wasn't until I heard the sirens that I came back to the front. That's when I saw her. Awful. Awful." He shook his head. "Well, I just stopped by to see how Douglas was holding up. Tell him I said hi and I'll stop by later."

"I will." Harrison assured him.

Slowly Wallace shuffled across the road back to his driveway. Harrison watched him and shook his head when he tried to imagine the old man running.

Turning around, Harrison looked at the gate. A knotted piece of rope was still tied to the gate post. He walked over to it and stretched to untie it but couldn't reach it. He made several attempts then stepped back and looked at it.

"There is no way," he muttered to himself.

He looked up at the crossbeam. Barbara's body was hanging in the center where their family sign had hung.

"No way," he repeated out loud.

He headed back to the house. *The coffee should be ready*, he thought.

Quietly, Harrison opened the back door and stepped into the dining room. The house was quiet. The scent of freshly brewed coffee filled the air. He turned and slowly closed the back door, making sure not to make a sound that would disturb Douglas.

With the door secure, he turned around and came face to face with a sleepy, teary eyed Douglas.

"Morning," he said once he caught his breath.

"Morning," Douglas answered with less enthusiasm.

"Coffee?"

"Thanks." Douglas sat down at the table. He leaned forward and propped his elbows on either end of his placemat and buried his face in his hands.

Harrison watched him from the kitchen. He knew a feeling like that, though he was sure Douglas would say it wasn't the same. When he lost his parents it was devastating. It felt as though his whole world had come to a stop and he wasn't even nineteen yet. Feelings of helplessness, abandonment and grief overwhelmed him but there was Danika to think about, to be strong for, so he buried those feeling and kept going. But Douglas was all alone. He had no one to think about or care for other than himself and that was what worried Harrison. It would be too easy for Douglas to give in to his feelings, grab the bottle and destroy himself in the process of mourning.

Harrison pulled the last two remaining unbroken cups from the cupboard, filled them with steaming hot coffee and joined Douglas at the table.

"Thanks," Douglas grunted. He wrapped his hands around the ceramic mug.

"I can fix us something to eat—"

"Don't bother. I mean, at least not for me. I'm not hungry."

"I understand," Harrison said and nodded. He took a sip from his cup.

"I guess I should call Barbara's parents," Douglas said in a distracted way. "What am I going to tell them?" His voice cracked and tears once again dampened his cheeks.

"Maybe you should wait until we hear from the sheriff," Harrison suggested.

"Wait for what? You heard Hanks. He'll convince Frank to say she killed herself."

"Then we'll fight it. There is no way she could have or would have done that. Not her. Besides, I just met your neighbor Wallace. There is something strange going on."

"What do you mean?"

Harrison recounted what Wallace had told him about the sound of a shotgun. He then told Douglas about seeing one behind the sofa and that it was gone when he went to move it back against the wall.

"I keep my shotgun in our bedroom," Douglas said and jumped to his feet. He headed for the stairs. Harrison followed.

Harrison had never gone upstairs, not even when he cleaned up the mess from the day before. He felt it would be a violation of his friend's privacy. However, since Douglas was leading the way he decided to follow, at least to the loft.

The bedroom door was open, the way the police had left it. Douglas went into the room headed straight for a tall gun cabinet against the wall to the left while Harrison hesitated at the threshold.

Looking into the room, Harrison was shocked. The bedroom had been torn apart. The king size bed was stripped bare, the pillows strewn on the floor. The dresser had all the drawers pulled out and emptied on the floor. Deep down, Harrison ached to go into the room and start cleaning if for no other reason, then for Barbara.

"It's gone!" Douglas shouted. "They took my goddamned shotgun. Those sons of bitches had no right!"

Harrison took a step into the room. "What?"

"I have the paperwork and serial numbers to prove that gun is legally mine." Douglas started rummaging through something in the bottom of a closet.

A feeling of déjà vu overwhelmed Harrison. Suddenly he was back home. His mother had just died. His father was upset about something, everything. He was restless and unfocused, stomping around the house, throwing out anything and everything that reminded him of his wife and at the same time getting upset that Harrison had moved a vase of flowers on the mantle.

It was happening all over again, only this time it was his friend. Harrison understood Douglas wasn't thinking. He was feeling, and the horror of his wife's death was fueling this semi-crazed hunt for his shotgun. Harrison remembered the behavior marked the beginning of a downward spiral for his father and his heart ached with the fear that Douglas was headed down the same road.

"Here it is!" Douglas announced. He stood up and shook the paper in his fist. "Come on, we're going to see Frank and get my gun."

Harrison followed Douglas down the stairs and out the front door. He paused long enough to lock it and then hurried over to the truck. Douglas had already started the engine by the time Harrison sat down in the passenger seat. The moment he closed the door, Douglas put the truck in gear and they were off.

"I can't believe they took my shotgun without telling me," he lamented.

Douglas parked on the side street and hopped out of the truck. He threw orange traffic cones, one in front and one behind the truck. "Company policy," Douglas said when he noticed Harrison's questioning expression. The two headed across the street to the courthouse. Harrison had to run to keep up with him.

Once inside the sheriff's office, Harrison expected Douglas to make a scene. Instead, he walked up to the counter and calmly and politely asked to speak to the sheriff. The young deputy smiled and told him to wait just a moment while she checked to see if he was available. A moment later she returned, following the man Harrison knew was the sheriff, Frank Porter.

"Douglas?" he sounded surprised to see him.

"Where's my shotgun, Frank. I have the paperwork right here. That gun was bought legally and is mine." Douglas held out the papers clenched in his fist.

Frank looked confused. "You better come into my office."

He held open the gate at the end of the counter for Douglas and Harrison before leading them down a hall to his office.

"Please, have a seat." He motioned to the two chairs in front of his desk while he walked around and sat facing them. "What gun?"

"My shotgun!" Douglas repeated a bit louder than he had said in the outer office.

"I'm sorry, I don't know what you're talking about."

Harrison could tell that Douglas was about to lose his temper. He sat forward and put a hand on Douglas's arm.

"Yesterday," Harrison spoke up. "When we entered the house, I saw a shotgun on the floor behind the sofa. After everyone left, the shotgun was gone."

"What's the gun have to do with anything?" the sheriff asked.

"I don't know, but I ran into Doug's neighbor across the

street this morning. He told me he heard two gunshots coming from the house. He said when he went to look he saw an Ellensburg police car parked alongside the road and figured they were already taking care of the situation."

Frank looked confused. He pulled a folder from the pile on his desk and opened it. Thumbing through the pages he started shaking his head. "There's nothing about that in this report. What's going on?"

"That's what I would like to know," Douglas snapped.

"Honest, Doug, we've known each other since you moved here. I'm just as much in the dark as you are. But I will get to the bottom of this."

"You might want to start with Chief Hanks," Harrison spoke up.

Sheriff Porter looked at him. "What's he got to do with this?"

"I don't know. But the other day a woman, Rosa, who worked at the Ocean Front Inn, was found dead in her home."

"How do you know this?"

"Because I spoke with her a couple hours before she was killed. I was supposed to meet her. Only, when Doug and I went to her home, the police and EMTs were there. Barbara was one of them. She told us that Rosa's injuries were not the result of stumbling in on a robber as Chief Hanks wants everyone to believe. Barbara was going to see what she could find out about what really happened. But if you ask me, I think the chief is behind it."

"That's a pretty serious accusation," Frank said and shook his head.

"I know. I also know he's driving my missing friend's Cadillac and he knows it too."

Frank's head turned sharply and his eyes registered

shock. "Are you sure?"

"Positive. Why else would he have done this to me and order me to leave town?"

Sheriff Frank looked at the bruises on Harrison's face.

"Frank, where's Barbara?" Douglas asked.

"Our coroner has her. He's determining the cause of death. Once I have his report, we can release her to the funeral home."

"Can you have someone else determine what happened?" Harrison spoke up.

"Well, I suppose I could see if the M.E. in Coos Bay could have a look."

"That would be great," Harrison said.

Frank looked at Douglas. "Is that what you want?"

Douglas looked at Harrison and then back at the sheriff. He nodded his head.

"Okay, I will make the call right away. And I will find out what happened to your shotgun."

"Thank you," Douglas said but he sounded a million miles away.

The two men stood up to leave but Harrison paused and turned back to face the sheriff.

"One more thing, when we walked into the house I noticed there was something smeared on the baseboards by the front door. Do you know what it was?"

Again Frank looked confused. "I have no idea. We were looking at it as a suicide, not a criminal investigation. I'm sorry, Doug. I will send a man out to have a look right away."

"That would be great," Harrison said and nodded.

When they reached the truck, Douglas grabbed the cones and stowed them in the back. Harrison climbed into the passenger seat and buckled the seatbelt.

"I need a beer," Douglas said when once again he climbed behind the wheel.

"The Port Hole?" Harrison asked.

"No. Let's just grab some at the store and go home."

"Sounds good."

CHAPTER THIRTEEN

Wednesday morning Harrison awoke to find Douglas lying on the bed next to him. In his morning after fog, he vaguely remembered Douglas saying something about not being able to sleep upstairs, in the bedroom where everything from the paint on the walls to the shams on the pillows reminded him of Barbara. They had retreated to Harrison's room where they proceeded to drink themselves into a stupor.

Harrison listened for a moment to Douglas' gentle snoring. Carefully and quietly, he slid from beneath the sheets. He grabbed his clothes from the floor and tip-toed to the bathroom. His head ached and throbbed.

He doused his head in the sink and grabbed the towel and dried off. His head still ached. After putting his clothes on, he made his way to the kitchen to start a pot of coffee.

Outside, a movement caught his attention. He jumped back and peeked around the cupboard through the back door. A man in dark clothes, with his face covered with a dark ski mask, stepped up to the door and tried the knob. He looked to his right and left before he began to pick the lock on the door.

Harrison's anger overcame his fear and he lunged at the glass door. The man let out a yell and fell backward onto the concrete patio. Harrison threw the door open and started for the would-be intruder. The man scrambled to his feet and took off around the corner of the house toward the street. Harrison gave chase.

When he reached the gravel road he saw the man jump into the passenger seat of an Ellensburg police car. The car then made a U-turn and sped away, throwing up loose gravel and a cloud of dust. Harrison retreated to avoid the cloud that moved toward him. Winded and still in shock, he made his way back to the house.

He checked on Douglas who was still sleeping off the ten bottles of beer from the night before. He hadn't heard a thing. Returning to the kitchen, Harrison started the coffee and tried to calm his shaking hands and nerves.

Harrison had just finished his second cup when a sleepy eyed Douglas wearing only his boxers stumbled into the dining room. His red hair, touched with grey, was mussed. A layer of fine red-blond hair covered his well-defined chest. *A lot has changed since high school*, Harrison thought quietly.

"'Morning," Douglas yawned. "What time is it?"

"It's nearly ten," Harrison answered. "How's your head?"

"Don't ask. Got anymore coffee?" He pulled out his chair and sat down at the table.

"Sure." Harrison jumped up and poured a cup. "You missed some excitement this morning."

"Oh?" Douglas asked and took a deep breath over his coffee cup before taking a sip.

"We had a visitor or I should say a burglar. At least I hope he was only here for something and not someone. I startled him before he could get in."

"Did you see who it was?"

"No. But, I did see his getaway car, an Ellensburg squad car."

Douglas's eyes widened. "No way," he gasped. He looked through the large window to his right at the side yard. "What is going on?"

"I don't know, but we must be getting close to finding out. That's the only thing I can figure."

Douglas shook his head and lowered his gaze. "But why did they have to kill Barbara?"

"Maybe she knew too much? I talked with her before we left for Coos Bay. She told me the gypsy camp was in the forest by the Hanks' land. She was going to take me to the camp so I could talk to that little girl again.."

"But how would whoever killed her know that?"

"I don't know," Harrison admitted.

"If only I had been home…"

"You can't do that to yourself. It's only natural to think that, I thought that about my parents. If only I had been able to, I don't know, stop my mother from getting cancer or stop my father from drinking himself to death. It's no use blaming yourself."

Douglas didn't look at Harrison. He kept his head bowed and closed his eyes. Harrison noticed the tears dropping onto the table.

"I'm so sorry," Harrison said and put his hand on his friend's shoulder.

After a shave and a shower, Harrison put on a fresh set of clothes. Douglas was waiting for him in the living room dressed in dark blue coveralls.

"Here," Douglas said then tossed a dark bundle at

Harrison.

Harrison caught it and unfolded the knit cap and dark blue coveralls. "What're these for?"

"Put 'em on," Doug answered.

"Why? What's going on?"

"We're going on a little spy mission of our own," he answered.

Harrison didn't need to ask where. He already figured it out. After pulling on the coveralls over his clothes, he stuffed the knit ski mask into his pocket.

The two secured the house before jumping into Harrison's rental car. "Less likely to be recognized," Harrison said. Douglas didn't object.

It took just fifteen minutes for them to reach the Indian Creek Café. Harrison parked the car in the lot.

"We go on foot from here," Douglas told him. He led Harrison down a service road that ran around the back of the café. On one side was the café and on the other, the forest's edge.

"We have to cut through the woods," Douglas said. "We don't want to take a chance on any of the Hanks spotting us. But be careful and follow me. I heard they've set traps out here to keep people away."

"I'll be careful," Harrison assured him. "Just don't go too fast. Remember, I'm a city boy now."

It took almost an hour before they reached Hanks' property line. A barbed wire fence marked the edge. Douglas followed without touching it to where it was secured to a post.

"It's electrified," he said pointing at the insulator. "I'm sure they have it hooked up to alarms or something. Be careful."

Slowly the two inched their way between the two lines

of wire. Once safely on the other side Harrison let out a quiet sigh. Douglas motioned for Harrison to follow and keep quiet, no talking.

Harrison didn't notice how long they'd been walking up hill. It was a gradual slope at first but then it became steeper. At points they had to almost climb vertically, helping each other to make sure neither fell or made a noise that would attract the attention of one of the Hanks' Dobermans.

"They keep them chained up near their house," Douglas informed Harrison. "When I was here doing some work I noticed a large metal building set quite a ways away from the barn and house. Little Sarah Hanks said it was her daddy's shop before Mrs. Hanks stepped in and told me to mind my own business and hurry up."

Knowing the dogs were chained up still didn't soothe Harrison's fears. If they were chained, they could be unchained and let loose easily enough, he reasoned.

When the shop came into view, Harrison realized that Douglas had led them around to the back of the property. The house was in the distance another hundred plus feet. Harrison spotted the dogs. They appeared to be napping in the sunlight near the front lawn.

They crept to the edge of the forest and ducked behind a large pile of firewood ready to be split. Harrison peeked over the top of the pile. The two-story metal building was huge, about the size of a four car garage and then some. Loud music blared from inside but didn't mask the sharp whining sound of a power saw cutting through metal. A dusty old window on the side that faced them seemed dwarfed by the size of the wall. Beneath it was what appeared to be the entrance doors to a cellar. A large metal strap spanned the width of the double doors and was secured by a padlock. Against the side of the building, running from the cellar doors to the back corner, was a chest-high row of neatly split and stacked firewood. Another shorter row was stacked between the pile waiting to be split and the building.

"They'll provide some cover," Douglas whispered and pointed. "Keep your eyes on that window to make sure no one sees us coming."

Carefully and quietly Harrison followed Douglas to the wood stacked against the building. Quietly they inched their way to the window and crouched down. They listened. The music was loud but they could still make out the sounds of men talking once the saw was turned off. How many and who they were, they couldn't tell. Cautiously, Douglas inched up and took a quick peek inside. Sitting back down, he turned to Harrison.

"There are three of Judd's sons, Bubba, Darin and Daniel, inside. It looks like they're running some sort of a chop shop."

Suddenly the music stopped. Silence fell over the shop.

"What have I told you boys about this racket?" Judd's voice thundered.

"Sorry, pa." one of the three boys answered.

"What are you doing? I told you I wanted that Bug dismantled."

"But, pa, we haven't got us a buyer for Volkswagen parts yet."

"My car," Harrison gasped. He stood up to take a peek. Across the shop near the large front doors, partially hidden under a tarp, Harrison recognized his Bug. He dropped back down and listened.

"I don't care. Get it done!" Judd snapped.

"No," Harrison quietly groaned.

"And what are you two still doing here? I thought I told you to take care of those two sons of bitches across the river or don't you care that they shot one of my officers?"

"We did pa," another son answered. "But Danny was almost caught."

"What do ya mean, almost caught?" Judd's voice continued to thunder inside the metal building.

"That houseguest feller saw me when I tried to get in. I panicked and ran," Daniel answered.

"Why didn't you just shoot him, ya good-for-nothing, waste-of …. Have you fed the cargo yet?"

"No pa'," Darin answered. "I'll do it right now."

"Not in your uniform! We don't need any of them recognizing you. Danny can do it. And for god's sake, put on your mask!"

"Yes, pa."

Douglas took a quick peek and then grabbed Harrison's arm. The two headed back across the clearing to the other wood pile. They ducked down just as Daniel came around the front of building.

"That was close," Harrison whispered. Cautiously he took a peek over the wood pile.

He recognized Daniel Hanks immediately. He was still dressed in the same black coveralls he wore when he tried to break through Douglas' back door. His ski mask was pulled up on his head, leaving his face exposed. What surprised Harrison was that Daniel looked nothing like his father. Daniel was tall, thin and lanky and not bad looking from what Harrison could tell. In his hands Daniel carried a tray covered by a white cloth. He set it on the top of the stacked wood and took a key from the pocket of his coveralls. He unlocked the padlock and opened the cellar doors.

"Here's your chow," he called out before pulling his mask over his face, picking up the tray and descending into the cellar.

"What kind of cargo needs to eat?" Harrison asked.

"I'm guessing it's probably people."

"What?"

"Yeah," Douglas answered and nodded his head. "Think about it. In the last three months at least seven men have gone missing, remember? Plus a while back I saw a 60 Minutes piece on a case of human trafficking in Seattle. It happened a few years ago. A group of businessmen were shanghaiing drunks from the local bars and selling them to foreign floating fisheries as cheap labor."

"Oh my God," Harrison gasped. "You don't really think…"

"I can't say for sure but that's my guess. Why else would Daniel need to wear a mask?"

Harrison rose up and took a peek just as Judd's son emerged from the cellar, the empty tray tucked under his arm. His ski mask once again pulled up, exposing his face. He secured the doors and headed back into the shop.

"What do we do now?" Harrison asked.

"Let's go."

"But we can't leave them," Harrison protested.

"We can't do anything about it now, it's too risky. If we get caught, who's going to help us?"

Harrison thought for a moment. Douglas was right. He nodded and followed Douglas back into the woods.

An hour and a half later, Harrison pulled into the parking lot of the Port Hole. The two headed inside for some lunch and a cold drink.

"I'll have a coke," Douglas told the waitress which

surprised Harrison.

"I'll have the same," Harrison said and handed the young woman the menu. He watched her return to the counter and post their order on the metal wheel in the window between the bar and the kitchen.

"I have to admit," Harrison spoke up. "I'm scared."

"That makes two of us."

"Do you think we should tell the sheriff?"

"Before we can tell this to anyone, we need to find out what's down there. We need proof."

"What sort of proof?"

"I don't know, but it has to be something irrefutable."

"Like what?"

"I don't know. You're the one who's supposed to be the detective." Douglas shrugged and shook his head. "Hey, Dani's a lawyer. She would know what sort of evidence we need. Give her a call."

Harrison pulled out his cell phone and speed-dialed Danika's number. The call went straight to her voicemail. "Dani, when you get this, call me. It's urgent." He ended the message and returned his phone to his pocket. "She must still be in court right now. I'll keep trying."

The waitress returned carrying two plates with a French Dip sandwich and a pile of fries on each. She set them down on the table and hesitated for a moment.

"Mr. Blair," she spoke quietly.

Douglas looked at her.

"I just wanted to say that I'm sorry about what happened to your wife."

"Thank you, but how did you find out?"

"I overheard a couple policemen talking about it. They were saying, something about her shooting a cop and how justice was served and the tax payers were spared the bill."

"Shot a cop? What cop?"

"I didn't hear them say."

"Do you know their names?" Douglas asked.

Harrison could tell that he was trying to mask the anger building inside him.

"I'm sorry, I can't say. I just started here and I don't want to lose my job. I just wanted to tell you how sorry I am. I met your wife when she came to my school and gave a talk during career week. She was really nice."

"Well, thank you," Douglas said dismissing her. "Call your sister when we get home," he said to Harrison before chugging his mug of coke as though it were a beer.

That evening, while Douglas sat nursing his third bottle of beer, Harrison slipped into the bedroom to call Danika for the fourth time. He was about to dial when his cellphone rang.

"Dani!" he answered. "Where have you been? I've been trying to reach you."

"I know. I got your messages. I was in court all afternoon and then in a meeting with my boss. What's going on?"

"Barbara's dead."

"Dead? Who?"

"Doug's wife, Barbara, she was murdered and the house was torn up and—"

"Slow down," Dani interrupted. "Start at the top."

Harrison took a deep breath and launched into an explanation of how they found Barbara.

"So, do the police have any idea what happened?"

"I heard the Chief of Police tell the Sheriff it was a suicide, but—"

"Was it?"

"No, it wasn't, Dani. She had bruises and scratches on her face, the same as I had when the chief slugged me. Plus, I talked to the neighbor and he said he heard gunshots. When he went to check it out, he said a police car was parked at the end of Douglas's driveway. Douglas lives in the county. There was no reason for a city police car to be there. Something isn't right."

"Harry, you've got to get out of there. This is too dangerous." Danika's tone sounded worried.

"I can't, Dani. Douglas needs me."

"Do you hear yourself? *Douglas needs me.* Harry, you don't have to take on everyone else's problems and fix them."

"But it's my fault."

"How is that?"

"If I hadn't come here—"

"Stop right there. Harry, I love you but you are out of your freaking mind. You cannot control what other people do."

There was a long pause. Harrison heard what she said but he also knew how he felt deep inside. *It was my fault, somehow.*

"Harry, I'm worried about you. You are three thousand miles away and I—"

"I know." he answered. He could tell she was about to cry. "Isn't there someone you can call? I need help. I don't trust anyone here."

"The minute we hang up, I'm calling the FBI office in Portland."

"Thank you."

"So, how's Douglas?" Dani asked.

"During the day he's been okay, sort of, but at night he stays up late drinking beer and then crashes on the couch. I'm worried about him, Dani. Remember dad?"

"Yes, but Harry, he's not dad.

"But he's my friend, Dani. I can't lose him, too."

"Okay," Danika answered after a long pause. "I'll make that call."

"But there's something else. Doug and I discovered who stole my car. It's the police chief and his sons."

"How do you know?"

"Because I saw it. They're operating a chop shop in a garage on their property."

"Please tell me you're not playing detective."

"Okay." Harrison teased but knew Danika wasn't playing.

"Harry, this isn't a game. This is serious. If these guys could kill someone they're not messing around."

"Well, how are we supposed to catch them?"

"You're not. Let me call the FBI."

"Wait, there's one more thing," Harrison interrupted her.

"Good God, now what?"

"I think they also kidnapped Thomas."

"What?"

"When we were there they took a large tray of food to someone or *someones* they have locked in the cellar beneath their garage. The police chief referred to them as cargo."

"Okay, I've heard enough. Let me make some phone calls and see what I can do. But promise me you will stay away from there, and you'll keep your friend away too." Danika's tone reminded him of their mother, same inflections and same sternness. In a flash he saw his mother's face and the scolding look in her eyes.

"Yes, mom," he answered before he realized it.

"Not funny," Danika answered. "I'll call you as soon as I find out what to do. Please be careful. I love you."

"Me too," Harrison answered.

"Bye."

Harrison looked at his phone and waited for Danika to disconnect the call, then placed it on the small side table next to the bed and returned to the living room to check on Douglas.

CHAPTER FOURTEEN

The sound of his cell phone ringing woke Harrison the next morning. He glanced over his shoulder and saw Douglas spread eagled across the top of the covers where he'd passed out the night before. It was becoming a habit. The sound of the phone didn't seem to bother him. Harrison answered the call while carefully slipping out of bed.

"Hello?" he whispered.

"What are you doing to find my son?"

Harrison groaned. He recognized Mrs. Unger's sharp tone. Quietly he tip-toed into the hallway and closed the bedroom door behind him.

"I'm still working on it—"

"Working on it!" she screeched. "It sounds to me like you're still asleep! It's nearly ten a.m. What have you found out?"

"Thomas was last seen in Ellensburg, Mrs. Unger. I'm here right now searching the area for him."

"What's taking you so long?"

"There's—"

"Never mind, I don't want to hear your excuses. I'm calling because my flight leaves in a half an hour."

"Flight? Where—"

"It's obvious to me you aren't getting anywhere so I'm flying up to Portland. I'll get to the bottom of this."

"They won't be able to help you there."

"So you say. Well, I will see for myself."

"When will you be arriving? I can have someone meet you and take you where you need to go."

"I'll be there about one."

"Okay, I'll make sure someone is there."

The call ended without any good-byes. Harrison's mind was reeling. He needed coffee but he also needed to get ahold of Justus right away. He quickly dialed Justus' number.

"Hi," Justus answered in his normal cheery tone.

"Justus, I need you to do me a favor," Harrison said getting straight to business. "Thomas' mother is arriving at the Portland Airport at one this afternoon. I need you to be there to pick her up and take her where she needs to go. Can you do that for me?"

"Uh, I think I can borrow my sister's car," he answered.

"Great. I don't know what flight she's coming in on but check when you get there for any flight arriving around one."

"I will but you do realize I'm at work."

"Oh crap! Fake an illness, you've got the sick time coming, don't you?"

"Yeah," Justus answered sounding like a total millennial. "But people have already seen me? They'll know I'm lying."

"Go into the men's room and pretend to throw up. Tell Eric or whoever, you're coming down with a cold or something. I don't know. You can think of something. This is an emergency. Please," Harrison said while he tried not to panic.

"Okay. I'll do it."

"Thanks, I'll owe you one." Harrison felt his body relax.

"I like the sound of that."

"Don't get too excited," Harrison warned. "Talk to you later tonight."

Harrison ended the call before Justus could say anything more. He took a deep breath and let out a relieved sigh. *One crisis diverted*, he thought.

While Harrison started the coffee, he heard the water turn on in the bathroom. Douglas was awake. Harrison opened the refrigerator and took out a bowl of eggs and the pitcher of milk. He scrambled them both a plate of eggs and made some toast. It was ready by the time Douglas was through with his shower.

"Morning," Douglas greeted, standing barefoot with a towel wrapped around his waist and another hanging over his shoulders. "Smells good."

Harrison smiled. "I thought we could use a little breakfast with our coffee this morning." He carried the two plates over to the table and set them down.

"Thanks," Douglas said and sat down in the chair across from Harrison. "Was that you on the phone?" he asked.

"Oh, you heard that? Sorry. I was trying to keep my voice down so you could sleep."

"Nah, don't be sorry. I wasn't asleep."

Sounded like it to me, Harrison wanted to say but didn't.

"Yeah, Thomas' mother called. She's flying to Portland to see what she can do. I tried telling her it was no use but…"

"Well, a mother's got to do what a mother's got to do." Douglas said and took a bite of his toast. "So, what's on the

179

agenda for today?"

"Do you have to work?"

"No, I told them about Barbara. They've given me some time off. Some guy from Grants Pass is taking over for me for a week and then I'll use a week of vacation."

"Well, I was hoping to hear from Dani this morning but—"

Douglas's house phone rang, interrupting their conversation. Douglas jumped up.

"Hello?" he answered. While he listened he turned to look at Harrison.

Harrison gave him a puzzled look.

"I see," Douglas said to the caller. He drew a star in the air with his finger.

Judd Hanks? Harrison mouthed the name.

Douglas shook his head. He covered the mouth piece and whispered, "Frank."

Oh, Harrison mouthed and nodded.

"Okay, we'll see you in an hour," Douglas said and then hung the receiver back on the wall phone base. "That was Frank. He wants to see us. Said he has some news about Barbara."

"Guess we know what we'll be doing today."

Douglas nodded. "I'll go get dressed. Thanks for the breakfast but I guess I'm not hungry after all."

"I understand. I'll clean up here and then take a quick shower myself."

Harrison watched his childhood friend walk over to the stairs. Douglas looked up at the bedroom door and hesitated before slowly starting up.

Minutes later, Harrison stood with his back facing the spray from the shower head. Slowly he tilted his head from side to side letting the hot water relax his stiff neck and shoulder muscles. It felt good to relax and have a moment to himself but a knock at the door reminded him he wasn't home.

"Yeah?" he called out.

The bathroom door opened and Douglas stepped inside. "Your phone was ringing. I think they left a message," he said.

Harrison turned the water off and pulled the plastic curtain open. Water dripped from his hair into his eyes.

"Can you hand me the towel, please?"

"Sure," Douglas answered.

Harrison groped blindly for the towel. Douglas put it into his hands. Harrison quickly dried his face.

"Did it say who was calling?" he asked and continued to dry himself.

"No, just said justice something."

"Oh no," Harrison groaned. He wrapped the towel around his waist and took the phone from Douglas. Justus had indeed left a message. He dialed the retrieval number and entered his security code.

"Hi, it's just me, Justus," Justus' cheery voice said. "I faked being sick so good everyone was afraid of me," he laughed. "I'm on my way to pick up my sister's car. I'll be at the airport in an hour or so. I just wanted to let you know so you don't have to worry. Bye for now."

Harrison erased the message and handed the phone back to Douglas.

"It was my house sitter."

"His name is justice?" Doug gave Harrison a look.

"It's spelled different but yeah."

"Who would name their kid that?"

Harrison shrugged. "Crazy people I guess."

Douglas shook his head. He turned to leave but stopped

in the doorway. "Do you ever think about when we were kids?" he asked without turning around.

"Yes. I do," Harrison answered.

Douglas turned his head and looked at Harrison. A faint smile spread across his lips. "Do you ever wish you could go back there?"

"All the time," Harrison admitted. "But it was a different time back then, a different world. So much has changed and I'm a different person because of it."

Douglas's gaze dropped to the floor. His expression seemed to mirror his feelings. For a moment, Harrison saw the boy inside, the serious, sensitive boy from so long ago. That is what drew them together as friends back then and that made it so easy to reconnect again.

"I haven't changed," Douglas spoke quietly. "I still..." He looked at Harrison. "I'll let you get dressed and then meet you outside."

Harrison watched the door close, leaving him alone in the bathroom once again. He stepped up to the sink and looked at his reflection in the antique mirror. "A lifetime," he said aloud and pushed the memory back into a dark corner of his mind.

Minutes later Harrison slipped behind the wheel of his rental car. He looked at his friend seated beside him and noticed that he had tears in his eyes. Gently he reached over the armrest and gave Douglas's hand a reassuring squeeze.

"It's going to be okay. I'm here and I will help you get through this."

Douglas didn't speak. He looked at Harrison and forced a smile, then gave a nod.

Harrison started the car, put it into gear and headed down the driveway. When he reached the street he suddenly slammed on the brakes catching Douglas off guard and causing him to lunge forward against the seatbelt.

"What?" Douglas gasped.

"The black car's back," Harrison answered and nodded in the direction of the neighbor's driveway across the street. He gripped the steering wheel tighter. He revved the engine. His eyes fixed on the black car.

Douglas turned in his seat, putting a hand on the dashboard to brace himself. "What are you doing?"

"I'm gonna ram that son-of-a-bitch!"

"What? No!" Douglas panicked. "They could be cops, remember?"

"I don't care."

"I do! We can't help Thomas if we're locked up."

Slowly Harrison eased his grip and relaxed his foot. He let out a sigh. "You're right."

Douglas sat back in his seat. "Just stay calm and drive slowly. If they're cops, don't want to give them a reason to pull us over."

"Okay." Harrison said and signaled for a left turn. He drove with one eye on the road ahead and one on the rear view mirror. His pulse quickened when he saw the mysterious car following them in the distance.

"Stay calm and breath," Douglas reminded him.

Harrison pulled up next to the curb across the side street from the courthouse. He sat for a moment, his hands still gripping the wheel, his knuckles white. The black car drove past on the highway behind them.

"You can relax," Douglas said trying to soothe his friend. "We're here and they're gone."

Harrison took a deep, quivering breath. He let it out slowly and at the same time took his hands off the wheel.

"I don't know why it upsets me so," he said to Douglas.
"I know."

Sheriff Porter greeted them when they walked into the outer office. Immediately he directed them to his office and closed the door behind them, locking it.

"I have to be very careful," he said. "Please have a seat."

Harrison and Douglas sat down in the chairs in front of the sheriff's desk. Frank sat across from them. He unlocked the lap drawer in his desk and took out a folder.

"I'll get right to the point. Yesterday I went to Coos Bay to see the M.E. in person. She's a personal friend of mine, so she agreed to examine Barbara's body for me," he explained. "You were right," he said and looked at Harrison. "Barbara did not kill herself. In fact, for the record, I never believed it either but in my position I have to wait until the facts are in before I voice my opinions."

Harrison looked at Douglas who sat with his hands clasped between his thighs, his jaws clenched. Douglas blinked his eyes rapidly to keep his tears at bay.

Frank flipped through the pages of the report. "She noted that she found residue on her face and hands that confirm she fired a gun, probably your shotgun." He looked at Douglas. "She also noted, as you saw, facial bruising and scratches consistent with being struck by a fist."

Douglas let out a soft gasp. His head began rocking.

"I'm sorry, I know this is hard to hear," his voice softened and his eyes reflected his sympathy.

Douglas nodded but didn't speak. He continued to rock himself slowly.

Glancing at Harrison, Frank continued. "There was evidence of a struggle. She fought her attackers."

"Attackers?" Harrison said out loud.

Frank looked at him. "Yes. There is evidence to suggest there were more than one."

"Oh my God," Harrison gasped. He looked at Douglas. Douglas' face turned red. Tears had begun to seep from the corners of his eyes. He was struggling. Harrison put his hand on Douglas's shoulder.

"Are you okay?" he whispered.

Douglas nodded but didn't speak.

"She must have hit one of them when she fired the shotgun. There were traces of blood on the soles of her shoes. Also, there was blood and tissue under her fingernails."

Harrison felt Douglas's body begin to quiver. He edged his chair closer. "Douglas, we don't have to do this," he whispered.

"No," Douglas answered in a faint, raspy voice that sounded like a wounded animal.

Harrison looked at the sheriff and nodded.

"Based on the bruising found on her neck, arms and legs, the M.E. concluded that Barbara was strangled, probably in the house. She didn't hang herself."

"Is there any word on the man she shot?" Harrison asked.

"No, the information has been passed on to their forensics team and they are still trying to get a match but if the person isn't already in the database..." Frank shook his head.

"Maybe you should talk to Chief Hanks," Harrison suggested.

"Why?" Frank gave him a puzzled look.

"Because he and his boys know who it is."

"And how do you know that?"

"Because we were heard them talking about Barbara

shooting a cop."

The expression drained from the sheriff's face. He rocked back in his chair, his mouth agape.

"How did you happen to hear that?" he asked.

Harrison looked at Douglas. Douglas was barely holding it together. His hands were trembling and his eyes were closed.

"Because we went out to his place yesterday," Harrison answered and cringed. "We heard them talking in their garage. But there's more—"

Frank halted him by putting up his hand. "Is this true, Doug?"

Douglas nodded.

Frank looked exasperated. "Now I don't know you from Adam," he said looking directly at Harrison. "We've just met, but Doug, come on. You know better than to break the law. I know for a fact, Judd Hanks has No Trespassing signs posted all around his property. You can't get close enough to his house, let alone his garage, unless you crossed that line."

"Well, can you get a warrant to search the garage?" Harrison asked.

"On what grounds?"

"On the grounds that Judd Hanks is driving my friend's stolen car."

"We'd have to prove it was stolen."

"His deputy told me—"

"It's hearsay, not evidence." Frank shook his head again. "I need something better to go on before I can get a judge to sign off on searching the city's top police officer's home."

"What if they were involved in kidnapping?" I asked.

"Again, I would need some sort of proof. Bring me that

and I will find a judge. But you have to do it legally."

Harrison gave a defeated sigh and slumped in his chair.

"I'm sorry, fellas, but my hands are really tied when it comes to deviating from the law."

"I understand," Harrison said.

Sheriff Porter looked at Douglas and his stern expression softened. "I'm not unsympathetic, guys. If I were in your shoes, I'd probably do the same; but just know trespassers do get arrested and sometimes even have to spend a night in jail and have to pay a fine, none of which sounds like much when it comes to saving a friend." He looked at Harrison and gave a slight nod.

"Thank you," Harrison said. Standing up he helped Douglas to his feet. Douglas pulled against Harrison's urging to leave and turned toward the sheriff.

"When will they release Barbara?" His voice was barely a whisper.

The corners of Frank's mouth lowered and his chin dropped slightly. "This afternoon," he answered. "Douglas, I'm so sorry."

"Thank you," Douglas nodded.

"Where do you want her taken?"

"I'll call Redwood Memorial and have them pick her up," Douglas answered and left the office.

"Thank you," Harrison said to the sheriff and hurried after Douglas.

The drive back to Douglas's house was quiet. Harrison kept checking the rear view mirror, watching the black car that was following them until they turned into the driveway. He didn't tell Douglas about the car. He didn't want to add to his stress.

"I'll call her parents," Douglas said after he unlocked

the front door and went inside.

"Do you want something to drink?" Harrison offered.

"No, I'll wait until after I talk with them."

Harrison walked into the back bedroom to give Douglas some privacy. However, with the acoustics of the log house, Harrison could hear every word. He tried not to listen but it was unavoidable, the house was too quiet.

The cell phone in Harrison's pocket vibrated and startled him. He had forgotten he silenced it before going into the courthouse. He quickly took it out and looked at the display. He tapped the green icon.

"Hi, Justus."

"The package has been received."

"What?"

"The *package* has been received," Justus repeated.

"Oh for the love of Pete, is she sitting there?" Harrison snapped.

"That is a big affirmative."

"Justus, knock it off. She is not someone you can joke around."

"Ooo, the dreaded mother-in-law—"

"I am *not* his mother-in-law!" Mrs. Unger's voice thundered. "How dare you suggest—"

"I'm sorry. I'm sorry. I was just teasing Harrison. I know your son is as straight as an arrow."

"My son's sexuality is not up for discussion. Just drop me at my hotel and let me out of this infernal rust bucket. Does your sister have a dog?"

"No, why do you ask?" Justus answered.

"Justus, please," Harrison pleaded with him. "No more horsing around. Just take her to her hotel and let her find her own way after that."

"Aye, aye, Captain."

The call disconnected. Harrison sat on the edge of the bed and stared at the telephone. It took him a few moments to realize that the house was quiet. He stood up and stuck his head into the hall and listened. Nothing. He walked back into the living room and saw Douglas sitting on the floor with his back against the sofa.

"Are you okay?" Harrison asked.

Douglas looked up. He took a deep breath and nodded. "I don't know what's worse, hearing what Frank said or telling her parents."

"There's nothing good about any of this."

"They asked to have her buried in the family plot in Yakima. So, I'll take her there when they have her ready."

"I can go with you," Harrison said without hesitation.

"No, you have to find Thomas. Barbara would have wanted that."

"We will and we'll catch whoever did this."

Douglas didn't respond. He turned his head and looked at the floor.

CHAPTER FIFTEEN

The sound of someone chopping wood woke Harrison. He turned over and looked at his watch. It was just after six in the morning. Harrison threw the warm covers off and climbed out of bed. The floor was cold against the bottom of his feet. He dressed in a hurry.

"Douglas?" he called out when he walked into the living room.

The sound of the chopping grew louder. Harrison looked out the front window. His mouth dropped open. He rushed outside. Just when he reached the driveway there was a loud crack. Harrison froze and watched the gate arch come crashing down.

To the right of the gate post, Douglas stood with sweat dripping from his brow even though it felt near freezing out. He leaned against the handle of his double-headed axe as if it were a cane.

"Douglas, what have you done?" Harrison asked stepping over the fallen arch.

"I couldn't stand looking at it another minute," he

answered. "I kept seeing her hanging there."

Harrison didn't say a word. He understood that feeling. After his father died, he went through the cupboards and poured out every bottle of liquor and smashed the empties in the bottom of the garbage can. It took years before he was able to look at a bottle, let alone drink any, without seeing his father in the hospital bed, bloated and dying. No, he understood the arch had to come down. It was a horrific reminder of Barbara's violent death.

"Coffee?" Harrison asked.

"Yeah," Douglas answered.

The two walked back to the house, leaving the fallen timbers blocking the drive. While Harrison started the coffee, Douglas slipped into the bathroom and washed the sweat from his face and the dirt from his hands.

Moments later, the two were seated at the table warming themselves with a cup of coffee.

"I think we should pay another visit to the Hanks' garage," Douglas said picking up his cup and taking a sip. "We need to find out who they're holding in that cellar." There was a subtle bitterness in his voice.

"I agree but shouldn't we wait for Dani to call back? She said she was calling the FBI for help; and she sort of made me promise to keep us both safe."

"To hell with safe," Douglas spat. "As long as Hanks is the chief of police in this town, there will be no justice. I'm sure he has every judge and attorney tucked safely in his back pocket. There's no chance of getting a search warrant, even if your sister was the head of the FBI or something. Even if Frank was able to, someone would tip Judd off. Frank and his men wouldn't find a thing. No, if we want justice, we have to take care of this ourselves."

Harrison had to admit that thought had already occurred to him. It kept him awake until well after mid-night. Still, taking the law into their own hands felt more frightening than what he imagined Judd Hanks would do to them if they were caught.

"So, what's the plan?" Harrison asked, and sipped his hot coffee.

"We wait until this evening, it's Saturday and Judd usually takes his wife to Coos Bay for dinner and a movie."

"How do you know that?"

"Because Barbara and I sometimes ran into them when we were there on our date-night," Douglas answered. "When we said hi, he mentioned they make it a weekly thing and even suggested we make it a double date. We never did." He looked out the window at the side yard. His eyes were red and damp with tears. "Anyway," he said and took a deep breath before taking another sip of his coffee. Harrison could tell Douglas was struggling. "With their parents gone, the boys will be hitting the pubs in town. They have quite a reputation around here."

"Sounds easy enough," Harrison said giving a nod of agreement. "But first we have to clear that driveway or neither of us will be going anywhere."

Douglas gave a thin smile, his first smile in days.

They finished their second cup of coffee and a store bought Danish before heading back outside. The sun had already begun to warm the air, taking the chill away. Douglas slipped around the end of the house and moments later came back with his chain saw and a spare pair of gloves for Harrison.

Harrison looked at the chainsaw and started to ask him why he hadn't used it instead of the axe but decided not to say a word. He slipped his hands into the heavy leather gloves. Douglas fired up the chainsaw and went to work, first cutting the crossbeam into small logs before moving on to the two support posts.

Harrison stood back and waited for Douglas to finish and shut off the saw. Watching him wield that motorized blade brought up memories of the crazed villain from the old horror show they had both snuck in to see when they told their parents they were going to a different movie. The title of that other movie had long been forgotten.

Once Douglas set the chainsaw down, Harrison began to gather up the wooden logs and stack them at the side of the driveway.

"I'll have Wallace come and haul it off later," Douglas had said.

By the time they finished, both were in need of a shower. Harrison's back ached. It had been years since he'd done this kind of work. Gently he took off the gloves while they headed for the house. Even with the added protection from the gloves, he'd still managed to smash his fingers between the logs from time to time.

"You can shower first," Douglas said when they reached the porch.

"No, you go," Harrison insisted. "I want to wait out here for a bit and cool down."

Douglas smiled again and then nodded. "Okay. I won't be long."

Harrison watched his friend walk back inside before he collapsed in the rocking chair in front of the living room window. His whole body ached but it felt good at the same time. Gently he rocked himself and let the cool air soothe his tired muscles. He pulled his cellphone out of his pocket and dialed Justus' number.

"Hi," Justus greeted in his normal perky tone.

"So, how did it go yesterday?" Harrison asked assuming Justus already knew it was him calling.

"Fine." Justus lowered his voice.

"Uh, why are you whispering?"

"Well, we sort of ran into a snag—"

"What?"

"I took your– Mrs. Unger to her hotel but it seems there was a mix up. They are having a comic book convention this weekend and quite a few of the attendees are staying at the hotel. Mrs. Unger took one look at some of their tight spandex costumes and, well, she refused to stay there."

"Where did you take her?" Harrison could feel himself beginning to panic. His mind started to envision the sort of places this *kid* would think of to take her. None of which were suitable for the wife of a minister in her mid-to-late sixties.

"She's staying in Thomas' room," Justus answered in a muffled voice.

"What?" Harrison shouted before he realized he'd raised his voice.

"I spent all afternoon running her around town. Every hotel we found that she was agreeable to look at was booked already. I've never known anyone pickier than her. What a b-word."

"So how did she end up in my house?"

"I told her it was late and I had to get back to feed Col. Mustard. So she sort of invited herself to stay here. She insisted on staying in Thomas' room. I'm sorry. I know the rules, no parties or having people over."

"Well, what's done is done. You did your best and I appreciate it. Thank you, Justus." Part of Harrison was relieved that she was there. At least he wouldn't have to worry about Justus breaking the rules.

"My sister said I can keep her car for the weekend. She's got her boyfriend's car. So, I will be able to drive Mrs. Unger around if she wants."

"Good. I really appreciate this."

"Oh! Gotta go. She's yelling about something."

"Okay."

Harrison ended the call and stuck the phone back into the pocket in his shirt. He rocked back in his chair and looked at the driveway. Even though the arch was no longer there, he couldn't erase the image of Barbara's lifeless body hanging in midair where it once stood. He stood up and went back into the house.

The sound of water running greeted him. Douglas was still in the shower. Harrison went into the kitchen and poured himself a cup of coffee. He put the cup into the microwave and heated it up. While he waited, memories of Douglas and him as boys flashed in his mind, memories of happier, carefree days. It seemed so long ago.

The sun was already casting long shadows of the trees across the parking lot by the time Harrison and Douglas reached the Indian Creek Café. Harrison locked his rental car and joined Douglas. They took the service road around the end of the building and slipped into the forest. Harrison tripped and stumbled several times before Douglas said they were deep enough to turn on their flashlights without being seen.

Even though it was dark, the trek to the border of the Hanks' land seemed shorter. They climbed over the barbed wire fence and made their way up the hill toward the garage building. Neither one said a word but Harrison could feel that this time something was different. This time they wouldn't run from any confrontation. Douglas had given him a baseball bat while he carried an old but heavy axe handle. Harrison thought it was silly because neither would be any defense against a gun.

"They won't have any guns," Douglas told him. "Judd doesn't allow it. I think because it's too traceable by forensics."

When they reached the clearing outside the garage, they crouched down behind the row of neatly stacked firewood.

"You sure you want to do this?" Harrison asked.

"We have to find out who's in that cellar. It could be Thomas," Douglas answered.

"Okay," Harrison nodded and turned to peek around the end of the row. Douglas rose up just enough to see over the top of the firewood.

In the distance the metal building, partially illuminated by a flood light high atop a pole between the house and the shop, stood silent. This time there was no loud music, no noisy saw. Harrison looked at the small window. It was dark. Suddenly Douglas grabbed Harrison by the arm and gripped it.

"The cellar," he whispered.

Harrison looked down at the cellar doors beneath the windows. In the dim light he could see it was unlocked and open. He turned back around and sat on the ground with his back to the wood pile.

"What do we do?" he asked.

"Well, let's have a closer look. One of us will stay up here and keep a lookout; the other will go down and check it out."

"I'll go," Harrison blurted.

Douglas gave him a confused look. "Why?"

"Because, if someone comes, you're better at swinging

a club than I am. I always struck out at baseball, remember? Another thing, if they lock me in down there, you could break me out."

"True," Douglas nodded.

Suddenly a distant memory and a feeling of déjà vu overwhelmed Harrison. He looked at Douglas and smiled.

"Just like old times," he reminisced. "Right, Batman?"

Douglas smiled.

"Back in a *Flash*," Harrison said and moved cautiously around the end of the firewood. Running as fast as he could, he darted across the open area to row of wood stacked against the side of the building and ducked down. From that distance he could see the open cellar doors. The lock lay open on the ground beside the doorway.

He listened.

Silence.

Harrison glanced back in Douglas' direction. In the darkness he couldn't see a thing. Feeling sure Douglas was still watching, Harrison crept over to the open door and looked in.

A set of wooden stairs led down to the cellar floor. In the dim light it was hard to make out much more. Harrison leaned down and cupped his ear to listen. There was no sound below.

Cautiously and quietly he stepped onto the top step. The board creaked slightly but held. Slowly he started down but immediately stopped when he was hit by a strong putrid odor. The memory of the dead possum he and Douglas found when they were boys flashed in his mind. The possum had been hit by a car and crawled into the shrubs behind Douglas' family's house where it died. With that memory came a wave of panic. It started in his legs and rose quickly to his chest and arms.

Harrison dropped the bat and grabbed for a handrail but found none. He teetered and almost fell.

Regaining his balance, he called out in a raspy whisper, "Thomas?" He pulled at neck of his shirt and covered his mouth and nose with it to filter the disgusting air. He stopped on the fourth step down and crouched low. He waited for his eyes to adjust to the darkness.

"Is anyone down here?" he whispered loudly.

No response.

He continued down the last three steps to the ground below. Staying crouched low, he repeated, "Thomas, are you here?"

No response again.

Slowly Harrison stood up and turned on his flashlight. The light illuminated the long narrow room. It was about twelve feet wide with timbered walls and heavy wooden beams overhead. The cellar stretched out about twenty or more feet in front of him. Harrison noticed a large dark spot in the dirt in front of him. He took a step back. His mind kept seeing scenes from all of the slasher movies he had ever watched. His breath caught as his fear grew. He turned the beam of his flashlight up toward the ceiling. A long narrow opening exposed the undercarriage of a car above him. He aimed his light at the floor again and felt the tension drain from his body. The spot in the dirt was motor oil. The room wasn't a cellar; it was an oil change pit. He felt his shoulders relax with the realization. *But what is that smell?*

He aimed the beam at the end of the room. A long, wooden workbench sat against the wall but there were no tools or anything else on it. He turned to head back to the stairs. When he did, the beam from his light flashed on something lying in the corner to the right of the stairs. Slowly he inched closer. His hand trembled causing the light beam to bounce on the figure. *Oh my God, is that a body?* His heart beat faster. The putrid smell grew stronger. Instantly he felt the warmth of adrenaline course through him. He fought his instinct to run and cautiously he inched his way closer to it.

"No!" he groaned when he recognized the shirt. "Thomas, no." He dropped to his knees beside the body and placed the flashlight on the bottom stair, aiming its beam at the body. Tears clouded his eyes. He wiped them away with his free hand; his other hand pressed the fabric of his shirt over his nose and mouth. Nervously he reached out to turn the body over to get a look at his friend. His hand shook and he pulled it back. *Stop it! It's just Thomas,* a voice in his head chastised him. He took another breath only to choke on the smell. Again he reached out but this time he took hold of the shoulder. It felt solid and cold. He pulled it toward him and the body rolled onto its back. Harrison let out a muffled scream. He fell backward onto his butt and quickly spider-walked away, keeping his eyes on the corpse. The disgusting air made him choke and gasp, his eyes blinded by tears. He pulled his shirt over his mouth and nose.

Once Harrison recovered, he inched back to look at the body again. "What?" he gasped and felt a strange feeling of relief. "You're not Thomas."

While the body was dressed in Thomas' clothes, it wasn't him. The face, mottled and splattered with dried blood, wasn't him. Half of the man's neck had been ripped away. Harrison's gut wrenched. He turned away and was sick. He wiped the spittle from his mouth and looked back at the corpse. The realization of the man's identity struck him. "Sergeant Hathaway," he said out loud. Grabbing the flashlight, he scrambled to his feet and up the stairs.

"Doug-las," he whispered when he reached the top of the stairs. He started for the woodpile and froze.

Three dark shadows rose up only feet from him.

"That's far enough," a deep voice said.

Suddenly Harrison was blinded by the beams from two flashlights. He ducked and covered his eyes. Stepping back he tripped and fell to the ground, his flashlight dropping from his grasp.

CHAPTER SIXTEEN

Standing in the glow from the flood lights in the parking lot of the Indian Creek Café, Harrison felt anger growing in his chest. He leaned against the side of a black Chrysler 300, the car that had been following them. Douglas stood beside him, his arms folded over his chest. It was clear to Harrison, Douglas felt the same irritation.

"Why were you following us?" Harrison demanded.

The two men, dressed in Dockers and casual, button front shirts didn't respond. They stood whispering to one another while keeping an eye on Harrison and Douglas.

"This is ridiculous," Harrison said. "Who are you?"

One of them, a buff, dark haired man with a strong, square jaw took a step closer but stayed out of arms' reach. He held up his hand, showing his ID. The other man held up his ID as well. He had what appeared in the dim light to be short blonde hair. He wasn't as buff as his partner but he was still intimidating.

"We're with the F.B.I.," he said. His voice was deep and intimidating. "I'm agent Haight and this is agent Becker. We know all about your missing friend and," he looked at Douglas, "we're sorry about your wife, Mr. Blair. Had we not followed you two to Coos Bay—"

"What's done is done," Douglas interrupted shaking his head.

Harrison knew, it wasn't that Douglas was okay with them not being there to protect Barbara. It was more that he didn't want to start down that avenue of What Ifs. Harrison knew that Douglas already blamed himself for leaving her that day and he wouldn't blame Douglas for blaming him as well. He did. Had he not come to Ellensburg, Barbara would still be alive. Harrison pushed his feelings down and tried to focus.

"You still haven't answered my question. Why are you following us?" Harrison demanded.

"Perhaps we should go inside. Would you care for something to drink?" Agent Becker spoke up. His voice was not as deep and sounded gentler.

Good cop, bad cop, Harrison thought and smirked. Still he looked over his shoulder at the glowing lights of the Indian Creek Café behind them. *It would be nice to sit down and have something to drink*, he reasoned silently.

The restaurant was quiet; the dinner rush had already gone. The four men took their seats around a small table that overlooked the parking lot. The agents took the seats with their backs to the wall leaving Harrison to sit beneath the window and Douglas with his back to the rest of the dining room.

The waitress, a nice looking young woman with long black hair pulled back in a ponytail, walked up to them with a smile.

"Good evening," she greeted and placed a single sheet menu in front of each of them. "Our special tonight is—"

"Nothing for me," *bad cop* barked.

"I'll pass, thank you," *good cop* said with a smile.

"I'll have a beer and cheeseburger," Douglas ordered.

"Make that just a root beer and scratch the burger," *bad cop* corrected and gave Douglas a stern look.

"I'll have a coke, instead," Douglas changed his order and glared at Agent Haight.

"I'll have the same," Harrison said. He waited until the waitress was gone before he turned to Agent Becker seated across from him.

"So, why have you been following us?" he demanded for the third time.

"We've been assigned to keep an eye on you so you don't interfere with our case," Agent Haight answered instead.

"Case?" Harrison repeated while he tried to understand. "You said you know about Thomas. Do you know where he is?"

The two agents exchanged glances.

"We do, but it's classified," Agent Becker answered.

"Classified? What's that supposed to mean?" Harrison's tone was blunt but he didn't care. His anger was beginning to return.

"It means, it's none of your concern," Agent Haight said.

"Bull shit!" Harrison yelled, his voice filling the diner as his temper reached a full boil. "Thomas lives with me. He's my friend. I look out for him."

"What my partner is trying to say is we can't tell you because it could jeopardize the case."

Harrison looked at them. His anger ebbed slightly. "Can you at least tell me if he's okay or not?"

"As far as we know he's alive," Agent Becker answered looking at his partner.

"Do you know where he is?"

"We have men watching them," Agent Haight took over.

"Is he safe?"

"That depends on what your definition of safe is," Agent Haigh responded again.

The waitress returned with their drinks and set them down in front of each of them.

"Can I get you anything else? Perhaps some hot wings?"

"That—"

"No, thank you," Agent Haight interrupted Douglas.

"Just let me know if you change your mind."

Harrison watched the waitress leave before looking at the two agents again. Their vague answers were beginning to grate on his nerves. He looked at Douglas who sat quietly taking sips from his glass. Harrison noticed that the muscles in Douglas's jaws were tight. It wasn't a good sign.

"So, what is this case you're working on?" Harrison asked.

"Why don't you tell us what you know," Agent Becker responded. "Maybe we can help put the pieces together?"

Harrison looked at Douglas. Douglas took the cue.

"We know that Hanks is running an elaborate chop shop. He uses his son's gas station and towing business in Port Orford to somehow scope out the cars. Then Judd Junior fixes them so they breakdown between there and Ellensburg."

"Interesting," Agent Haight said. His expression gave no clue as to whether or not Douglas' assessment was accurate.

Douglas glanced at Harrison. Harrison nodded, urging Douglas to keep going.

"Was the body they took from the cellar the cop—"

A buzzing sound interrupted Douglas. Agent Haight hastily reached into his pocket and pulled out his cellphone. He looked at it; presumably reading a text message, then stuffed it back into his pocket and leaned toward his partner.

"We've gotta go," he said. He looked at Harrison and Douglas. "That means you too. Come on."

"Wait a minute," Harrison protested. "Where are we going?"

"Never mind, you're coming with us so we can keep an eye on you," Agent Haight sneered. "So, pick it up! We gotta hurry."

Harrison took one last gulp of his coke while he stood up. Agent Haight had already started for the door with Douglas behind him. Agent Becker waited for Harrison and then hurried him along.

Once outside, the two agents headed for their Chrysler. Harrison started for his rental.

"Where do you think you're going?" Agent Haight snapped at him.

"My rental."

"Leave it. Get in." He opened the back door their car. "Move it!" he commanded when Harrison hesitated a moment.

"You can pick up your rental car later," Agent Becker said while he ushered Harrison into the back seat and closed the door.

Agent Haight didn't wait for them to buckle up before he put the car in gear and held the gas pedal to the floor. The car made a violent and sharp turn to the left back onto the road leading back into Ellensburg. Douglas fell against Harrison.

"Hey, what's the hurry?" he shouted his disapproval.

"Tell the Coast Guard to stand by," Haight told his partner, ignoring the two in the backseat. "Have our guys close in but wait for us before they confront them."

"Got it," Becker answered and relayed the message to the person on the other end of the cell phone call. "They're at the docks and waiting," Agent Becker announced.

"The docks? Coast Guard? What's going on?" Harrison asked while he continued to be jostled around even though his seatbelt was now secured.

"Good." Agent Haight responded to his partner while he continued to ignore Harrison. "Let them know we're five minutes out."

Harrison looked at Douglas. "It sounds like our theory about shanghaied men and fishing boats might be valid."

"That's what I was thinking," Douglas answered. He, too, was holding onto the armrest in the door with one hand and the back of the front seat with other. "I think we're headed for some sort of show down."

"Doesn't this thing have a siren and lights?" Harrison asked while he continued to be buffeted around in the back seat.

Agent Becker turned his head. "No. Besides, we don't want to alert them until the last minute."

Harrison shifted in his seat to get in a more stable position.

When they neared the intersection with the bridge, Agent Haight didn't slow down. He crossed into the oncoming lane and Harrison could have sworn the car went airborne when Haight pulled back onto Highway 101.

Once they reached the Harbor Way on the right, Haight cranked the steering wheel. The car turned sideways causing Harrison to fall over onto Douglas' lap.

"Hang on!" Becker shouted over his shoulder.

The car fishtailed. Harrison thought they were going to

roll. Then Agent Haight gained control of the car and slowed it down but still drove over the speed limit. They passed the Port Hole and then Haight slammed on the brakes. Harrison and Douglas lunged forward.

Once the car stopped, the two agents threw their doors open.

"Stay here!" Haight barked. The doors slammed shut behind the two agents.

Harrison looked between the headrests on the back of the front seat and watched them disappear down the ramp toward what he assumed were the dock. "Like hell I will," he said and opened his door. Climbing out, he ducked around the back of the car and opened the driver's door.

"What are you doing?" Douglas asked.

"I'm not good at sitting around and doing nothing. If they've got my friend, I'm gonna help." He popped the trunk open.

Douglas scrambled out of the backseat. Harrison grabbed the tire iron and closed the trunk.

"Fine, this way," Douglas said.

Harrison followed Douglas as he stealthily ran over to the alleyway between the small marina office building and the steakhouse next door. Steam from the restaurant's vent blew into the alley and created a fog in the cold night air. Douglas ignored it and led Harrison past to the boardwalk on the other side.

They stopped when they reached the end of the marina building. Douglas pressed his back against the outer wall. Harrison did the same. Douglas motioned for Harrison to be quiet and stay put. Then he peeked around the corner of the marina. Without warning, he darted across the boardwalk to a large concrete planter and ducked behind the decorative evergreen tree planted in it.

Harrison moved over to the corner of the marina and looked up and down the boardwalk. It was as impressive as some of the malls in Portland. Benches and decorative trees and plants in huge concrete planters adorned the rustic, wooden boardwalk. A three foot high, iron fence with cutouts of anchors and starfish protected people from slipping off the walk and into the harbor waters below. The fence was topped by a smooth pipe handrail.

"Come on!" Douglas whispered and motioned for Harrison to join him.

Harrison ducked and ran across the boardwalk.

Douglas raised up a bit and looked over the top rail. Harrison looked through one of the cut outs.

In the glow from the lights at the tops of the lampposts that lined the pier, Harrison spotted the agents and their men. They appeared to have their guns drawn and were closing in on a large charter boat at the end of the pier.

"There," Harrison said giving Douglas a nudge and pointing.

Suddenly loud popping sounds rang out, echoing off the water and the cliff on the north side of the Rogue River. Harrison and Douglas ducked down.

"Oh my God, is that gunfire?" Harrison gasped.

Douglas didn't answer. He kept his back to the metal fence. He waited until the shots subsided before he turned around and took another look.

Harrison looked through the cutout again before venturing a better look over the top of the rail.

The agents had boarded the boat. On the pier lay what looked like two men in dark clothing. Harrison wasn't sure if they were their agents or two others. His stomach tightened with worry.

Just when the shooting started to die down, Harrison caught sight of the dark shape of a man emerging from between two nearby boats. It headed for the ramp. Even without the benefit of light, Harrison knew who it was. His hands tightened around the tire iron. His teeth clenched. He watched the figure scurry up the ramp and head toward them. Harrison's heart pounded.

It happened so fast. The shadow came closer. Harrison stood up and swung the tire iron with all his might. The iron hit the man across the chest, knocking him to the hard boardwalk. He landed with a thud. Harrison raised the tire iron again while he stood over Chief Hanks.

"Don't move!" he ordered the police chief.

Judd lay flat on his back, winded and in pain. He looked to his sides. When the tire iron struck him, he let go of his firearm. It skidded across the wooden boardwalk and onto the pavement, out of reach.

"Get his cuffs," Harrison ordered.

Douglas hesitated a moment and then did as Harrison said. Thankfully the chief had his cuffs hooked on his left hip.

Judd lay still, his hands raised up in case the iron came down on him again, but once Douglas tried to cuff him, he grabbed Douglas' arm and tried to use him as a shield as he leveraged himself to his feet.

"Oh, no you don't!" Harrison said. His grip tightened. He waited until he had a clear shot at the chief. He closed his eyes and swung with all his might. There was a sound like a watermelon hitting the ground and splitting open. Then silence.

Harrison opened his eyes and saw the police chief lying on top of Douglas, blood oozing out of a gash in the side of his head. Stunned, Harrison dropped the iron.

"Doug?"

"I'm okay," Douglas groaned. "Get him off me." He pushed against the dead weight of the cop, rolling him off and onto his back.

Harrison helped Douglas to his feet.

"I see your batting average has improved," Douglas said with an approving nod.

"Is he—"

Douglas reached down and felt for a pulse. "Nah, he's just out. Although, I imagine he's going to have one hell of a headache when he wakes up."

"I thought I told you two to wait in the car?" Agent Haight said, Becker close behind him.

Harrison ignored the words and heard only the relief in the agent's voice. "Well, what can I say?" He shrugged.

The four men stood back and watched the EMTs load the chief onto a gurney. No one said a word. Becker bent down and picked up the tire iron. Once the EMTs were on their way, the four headed back to the car.

CHAPTER SEVENTEEN

Harrison stood and watched the flashing lights of the emergency vehicles bounce off the façade of the marina office and neighboring steakhouse building. When the last ambulance sped off, throwing gravel in its wake, he turned toward the agents.

"So, what happened down there? We heard the gunshots."

Becker looked at Haight and after some subtle nonverbal cue was exchanged, said, "Seems Chief Hanks and his men weren't going down without a fight. They fired on us and we returned fire."

"Was anyone hit? Those two men on the dock?" Douglas asked.

"There were a few injuries and regretfully, casualties."

Harrison felt his strength drain from his body. His legs became weak and he steadied himself against the side of the car.

Douglas glanced at Harrison and their eyes met briefly.

"Did you find Harrison's friend, Thomas?" he asked.

"Was he…"

"We can't say until the families of the victims have been notified," Agent Haight answered.

"Come on," Douglas said. "We're on the same side here."

"Procedures," Haight shrugged.

"Screw you!" Douglas spat.

Harrison looked at Douglas. Douglas' eyes widened. His mouth moved as though he were saying something and he started around the end of the car. Darkness moved in from the edges of his vision and suddenly he was falling, his connection to his body disappeared and maybe that was lucky. When he next opened his eyes he was sitting on the parking lot pavement, slumped against the Chrysler. A man with a small flashlight was shining it in his eyes.

"He's going to be fine," the man said. "He just fainted."

Fainted? Is that what that was? Is that what if feels like?

"Thank you," Douglas said.

The two ambulance attendants left.

"Think you can stand?" Douglas asked and took Harrison's arm.

"I think so."

Slowly and gently, Douglas helped Harrison to his feet. Harrison continued to lean against the side of the car until he felt sure his legs would hold him again.

"Are you okay?" Agent Becker asked, sounding truly concerned.

"I think so," Harrison repeated.

"Good," he said with a pleasant smile. "The men the Hanks were holding have been taken to the Port Hole. We're in the process of identifying them. Some were drugged pretty heavily," the agent explained. "How about we all go over there now? You can rest a bit and get something to drink."

"A beer this time," Douglas said looking directly at Agent Haight.

The agent hesitated a moment and started to nod his head. "Why not?"

With Harrison holding onto Douglas' arm for support the four men made their way around the steakhouse and across the parking lot to the Port Hole. Harrison was surprised by the number of fire engines, rescue trucks and squad cars there were parked in the lot. He didn't remember hearing any of them.

Inside the Port Hole, Harrison was hit by the loud noise of several people talking at once. He looked toward the back of the restaurant by the bathrooms. The tables had been moved around and what appeared to be a mob of men and women in white shirts with patches and men in orange were huddled together.

"We'll have a seat over here," Agent Becker said to the hostess who appeared to be a nervous wreck.

"That would be good." She tried to smile but it looked as though she was about to cry. "Can I get you anything to drink? It may be a while before we can get you something to eat."

"A drink is fine," Agent Haight assured her. "Four beers."

"Make that, three beers and a rum and coke," Douglas corrected and glanced at Harrison.

Once they were seated in the opposite corner away from the commotion, Agent Haight looked at Douglas and took a deep breath.

"Just what do you two know about what was going on

here?"

"Nothing really, I mean, we have our suspicions," Douglas answered.

"Well, I'd be interested in hearing them," Haight said.

"Here we go," the hostess returned with her tray with three mugs of ice cold, golden beer and one tall glass of rum and coke. She set them on the table and let the men decide which one they wanted. "If you need anything else, I'll be at the bar."

Harrison watched her leave. The three other men grabbed a mug each and took a large gulp before settling back in their chairs.

"My guess," Douglas resumed their conversation, "Chief Hanks was the mastermind behind an elaborate scheme. He used his office and position to ensure that no one would discover what he was doing on the side. He used his son's gas station and the Ocean Front Inn where his daughter works to scope out and to kidnap men to sell to foreign fish processing vessels. Slave labor."

"Really?" Haight said and took another gulp of his beer.

"We know that Thomas' car broke down at the viewpoint just north of town, the same place that Harry's VW died, because we found the discarded license plates. Hanks and a couple of his other sons ran a chop shop to dispose of the cars.

"We know that Thomas stayed at the Ocean Front and the next day Hanks' daughter burned up his things. We suspect it was one of them who killed Rosa, the maid, because she knew too much."

"So what gave them away?" Becker asked.

"Hanks got sloppy and kept Thomas' Caddy. Harry spotted it and put two and two together."

"Not bad," Becker nodded and looked at Haight.

"You two are very perceptive. Ever thought of becoming detectives?" Haight asked.

"So, we were right?" Douglas asked.

"I can't say."

"Of course not," Douglas smirked and took a gulp of his beer.

Just then Sheriff Porter walked up. He took a look at Harrison and Douglas and smiled. "Figured I see you two here," he said.

"Well, we did have help getting here," Harrison spoke up and nodded in the direction of the agents.

"Yeah, I know. Agent Haight and Agent Becker paid me a little visit after you left the other day. They wanted to know what you both were up to. They also filled me in on their investigation. And it was a good thing they did. I was about to get a warrant which would have tipped Hanks and his sons off."

"What about the blood?" Douglas asked. "Any news on whose it was?"

The sheriff nodded. "Yes, it was one of Hanks' men, a Sergeant Hathaway."

Harrison and Douglas looked at each other.

"What about the other guy, the one she scratched?"

"That was another one of his men. We found his body on the beach north of Ellensburg," Frank continued.

Harrison shook his head. "Why? Why did they go after Barbara?"

"I honestly don't know and I don't know if we will ever know for sure. Two of Hanks' sons, Bubba and Darin, were killed in the shoot-out tonight, and I hear you worked over ol' Judd pretty good." He looked at Harrison. "He's still unconscious and it's too early to say if there is any brain damage. But, my guess is they were trying to scare you away but you weren't home. Instead they came face to face with Barbara when they broke into the house. That's when things went horribly wrong. I know it's no consolation. I don't think they set out to kill Barbara or hurt anyone."

Douglas pushed away from the table and stood up. He walked a few feet away and kept his back toward the four.

Harrison's heart ached for him. He looked back at Frank. "What about Thomas? Is there any news about him?"

"The men they were holding are over there. If you like you can have a look and see if he's among them."

Harrison hesitated for a moment, glancing at the gathering across the dining room and then back at the agents and sheriff. He gulped down the last of his rum and coke. "Sure," he answered.

Slowly he stood up. His legs felt like they were made of rubber but they were holding up. Deliberately he walked around the other tables and made his way across the room.

The men were seated. The few that had already been looked over were lined up on chairs by the outer wall. A few were being examined by the medical teams set up at some of the tables. The men appeared to range in age from their late teens to early thirties. They were from different races, Asian, African-American, Hispanic, and Caucasian. Harrison noticed one young man hunched over at the end of the line. A blanket was draped over his shoulders. His shaved head was turned away. His hands were clasped between his knees while he rocked back and forth. There was something familiar about him. Harrison walked over and knelt down in front of him.

"Thomas?" he said softly.

The man turned his head. His brown eyes looked at

Harrison without any sign of recognition.

"Thomas, it's me, Harrison."

Slowly the man stopped rocking. He reached out his hand and touched Harrison's face, felt his hair. His eyes became glassy with tears.

"Harry?" Thomas' voice was thin and raspy.

"Yes, Thomas, it's me. I'm here." Tears began to stream down Harrison's cheeks.

Suddenly Thomas lunged forward and wrapped his arms around Harrison and held on. Harrison felt Thomas' whole body tremble while he hugged him.

"Thank God, I've found you," Harrison cried.

Three hours later, back at Douglas's house, Harrison walked into the living room.

"He's sleeping finally," he whispered to Douglas. "He didn't want me to close the door."

"I don't blame him." Douglas interjected. "After being locked in that hell hole for two weeks or more, being beaten and drugged and nearly starved..."

"I can't think about that," Harrison shook his head and held up his hand. "It breaks my heart."

"He's going to need counseling, you know. And even then, he's not going to be the same person you knew."

Harrison sat down at the dining table. He had always thought that once he found Thomas they would go back to their lives in Portland. Things would resume the way they had been. Thomas would go back to his job at Nike and everything would be okay. This would all be a bad dream.

"Have you called his mother?"

"No. Not yet. I thought I would wait until morning. There's nothing she can do tonight."

"True," Douglas agreed. He looked around the room. "So, you'll be leaving soon?"

"I suppose I will although I hate to leave you."

"I'll be okay."

"I can't help but think this is all my fault—"

"Don't." Douglas interrupted, "don't even start that kind of talk. Barbara and I wanted to help you. We have been sick of the way the town has gone to the dogs since Hanks took over as chief of police. This has nothing to do with you."

"Still, if I—"

"No!" Douglas snapped. "You don't get to do this to yourself. Not every bad thing that happens is because of something you did. I know you still blame yourself for your mother getting cancer, for your father's drinking himself to death. Harry, bad things happen all the time, to even the best of people. What happened to Barbara is not your fault. She was just in the wrong place at the wrong time. I'm just glad she got one of those bastards."

"Do you believe that?" Harrison asked.

"Yes, I do. I do now," Douglas said sounding more sure with every word. "So, you can go back to Portland and not give it another thought. No regrets."

"If you say so," Harrison said though deep down he still felt as though what happened to Barbara, to Rosa, even those men, was the result of his failure somehow.

"I do say so," Douglas answered. "Now, we should get some sleep."

"I'll just sack out on the couch."

"Sure? There's plenty of room upstairs," Douglas offered.

"I think I need to stay close, in case Thomas wakes up and needs me."

Douglas smiled. "Still taking care of everyone," he laughed. "Night." Before leaving Douglas gave Harrison a hug. "I love you, Harry."

"Me too."

Harrison watched Douglas walk up the stairs to his bedroom. He smiled to himself and thought how good it felt to reconnect with his old friend.

Slowly Harrison walked over to the sofa and sat down. He pulled the blanket around his neck and rested his head on one of the small sofa pillows.

CHAPTER EIGHTEEN

The sun was bright and nearly straight overhead. Harrison closed the door on his new burgundy Honda CRV and took a deep breath to settle his nerves. He glanced at the sign by the walk, Terrace Heights Memorial Park Visitor Parking Only. He tugged at the collar of his shirt to loosen it a bit and let the breeze cool him. *Why did I have to go and wear my black suit?* he silently regretted.

Heading off, he made his way around a picturesque pond with its manicured flower and shrub beds and fountain that sprayed water ten feet into the air. Across the lush green lawn, beneath a flowering ornamental cherry tree a large crowd gathered. For a moment Harrison thought about hanging back and waiting until it was over but thoughts of everything Barbara had done for him came flooding back and motivated his feet to keep walking. Besides, he promised Douglas that he would be there.

As discreetly as he could, he slipped in between two women at the back of the gathering. Over the heads of the people in front of him he could see the beautiful cherry wood coffin partially draped in a white cloth and laden with a colorful bouquet of pink roses and pink carnations.

A priest, the same one from the church, stood at the head of the casket. A small boy in his altar boy uniform stood dutifully at his side holding a small brass bucket with Holy Water inside.

Memories drowned out what the priest said. In his mind's eye Harrison saw his mother's casket. The powder blue cloth covered wooden box his father insisted was all they could afford. A small bouquet of white roses tied together with a blood red ribbon lay on top. The priest mumbled and waved a brass shaker, sprinkling water on everyone and the casket. Harrison didn't hear a word then either. Still he managed to say amen when the rest of the gathering did.

The priest walked over to Douglas and his in-laws and shook their hands before leading his mini-me away. Harrison held back and waited for the crowd of friends and family to disperse and for Douglas to be alone.

Douglas bent down and whispered something before kissing the coffin. When he looked up his eyes met Harrison's and he smiled.

"You made it," he said and rushed over to him.

The two hugged. "I was afraid it was too soon and you wouldn't be able to get away."

"I wouldn't miss it." Harrison answered and held onto Douglas a little longer. "How are you doing?" asked when they finally parted.

"I've had better days but at least now I can move on." The two started across the lawn toward the parking lot. "Oh, you will be happy to know that I've applied for a job in Portland and have put my house on the market."

"You have?"

"Don't sound so surprised," Douglas laughed. "I was raised in the big city, remember?"

Harrison chuckled. "Yeah, but your house and property, they're so beautiful."

"Not without Barbara. Besides, I don't have many friends in that town, just acquaintances and clients really. All of my *friend* is in Portland."

Harrison smiled. He understood what Douglas meant and it even made him blush a little.

"So, how are things with you? Work going good?"

"Oh yeah," Harrison grinned. "Thanks to Justus and his emails, Corporate came in and cleaned house. Trouble making Debra found herself unemployed and the little boss man who couldn't keep it in his pants was offered a nice severance package or termination. He opted for the package. I don't really care. He's gone."

"That's great news," Douglas answered and put his arm around Harrison's shoulders while they walked. "How's Thomas?"

Harrison stopped. The smile faded a bit from Harrison's lips and he looked at the ground while he gathered his thoughts. "Thomas has moved back home with his parents."

"He has? Why?"

"You were right. He needed more help than I could give him, and with his mother waiting when we got back to Portland, she took over. She packed up his things and they flew back to San Diego."

"Harry, I'm so sorry."

"It's okay," Harrison shook his head. "He needed a change of scenery and the support of his family."

"Still, after everything you did, that has to sting a bit."

"It does, but I'll survive. I already have a new border.

Remember my house sitter, Justus?" Harrison laughed.

"Yeah," Douglas answered sounding a bit skeptical. "How's that going to work out? I mean, working with him all day and then having him there when you go home?"

"I don't know. For now, it's okay but time will tell. He's quite the kid."

"Well, don't rent out your other room. Who knows, I just might come knocking, myself."

"The door's always open."

ABOUT THE AUTHOR

Author A. M. Huff was born and raised in the Pacific Northwest. At an early age he aspired to be a writer and over the next thirty years, he continued to write with the encouragement of friends and relatives.

After retiring early from his day job, he joined a writers group and began down the path to publication. *Ellensburg* is the first of a series of suspense/thriller novels.

For more about A. M. Huff visit his website: amhuff.com

If you've enjoyed this story, please leave a review on Amazon.com or Goodreads.com.

53272827R00134

Made in the USA
San Bernardino, CA
12 September 2017